MEDICAL ETHICS

ISSUES FOR THE 90s

DRUGS IN AMERICA
by Michael Kronenwetter

MANAGING TOXIC WASTES
by Michael Kronenwetter

**MEDICAL ETHICS:
MORAL AND LEGAL CONFLICTS
IN HEALTH CARE**
by Daniel Jussim

THE POOR IN AMERICA
by Suzanne M. Coil

THE WAR ON TERRORISM
by Michael Kronenwetter

ISSUES FOR THE 90s

MEDICAL ETHICS

Moral and Legal Conflicts
in Health Care

Daniel Jussim

JULIAN MESSNER

AP/Wide World Photos: pp. 40, 67, 91. Mark Artman/The Image Works: p. 15. Brown Brothers: p. 26. Alan Carey/The Image Works: p. 24. Custom Medical Stock Photo: p. 73. © 1989 Catherine Smith/Impact Visuals: p. 103. Jim Sulley/The Image Works: p. 60.

Copyright © 1991 by Daniel Jussim.
All rights reserved including the right of
reproduction in whole or in part in any form.
Published by Julian Messner, a division of
Simon & Schuster, Simon & Schuster Building,
Rockefeller Center, 1230 Avenue of the Americas,
New York, NY 10020
JULIAN MESSNER and colophon are trademarks of
Simon & Schuster, Inc. Design by Claire Counihan.
Manufactured in the United States of America.

Lib. ed. 10 9 8 7 6 5 4 3 2

Library of Congress Cataloging-in-Publication Data

Jussim, Daniel.
Medical ethics: moral and legal conflicts in health care / Daniel Jussim.
p. cm.—(Issues for the 90s)
Summary: Examines current controversies in medical ethics, including issues such as abortion, organ transplantation, euthanasia, and health care for teenagers, the critically ill, and AIDS patients.
1. Medical ethics—Juvenile literature. [1. Medical ethics.]
I. Title. II. Series.
R724.J86 1991
174'.2—dc20
90-33450
CIP
AC

ISBN 0-671-70015-4 (lib. bdg.)

ACKNOWLEDGMENTS

Thanks to the following people for their help: Bruce Jennings, Ann Oplinger, and Judith Jussim reviewed the manuscript; Carol Barkin edited it; Cheryl Solimini copyedited it; and Marta Howarth, librarian at the Hastings Center, provided valuable material. Several organizations also contributed important documents; they are listed with their addresses at the end of chapters 2, 4, and 6.

CONTENTS

ONE **MORAL VALUES IN HEALTH CARE**   1

TWO **ABORTION AND TEENAGERS**   10

THREE **WHO SPEAKS FOR THE TEENAGER?**   21

FOUR **REPRODUCTION**   36

FIVE **CRITICALLY ILL BABIES**   57

SIX **CRITICALLY ILL ADULTS AND THE "RIGHT TO DIE"**   64

SEVEN **ORGAN TRANSPLANTS AND ECONOMICS**   85

EIGHT **THE DOCTOR-PATIENT RELATIONSHIP**   96

NINE **RECURRING THEMES**   110

Appendix: **LANDMARK COURT CASES**   115

INDEX   119

CHAPTER ONE

MORAL VALUES
IN HEALTH CARE

KAREN was sixteen when her kidneys failed. The doctors' attempts to restore the young woman to health by transplanting one of her father's kidneys into her body were unsuccessful. Now she can be kept alive only by dialysis, a process in which a machine filters toxins from the blood. The dialysis can keep her alive indefinitely, but it causes Karen great discomfort—chills, nausea, vomiting, bad headaches, and weakness—and she says she would prefer to end the treatment and die peacefully.

Her parents support this decision, but her doctors resist. Like all physicians, they are committed to keeping their patient alive. It is against their every instinct to just let so young a person die.

Conflicts like this one (discussed fully in Chapter 3) used to be rare. Before the introduction of sophisticated drugs and medical equipment in this century, doctors could not offer their patients much besides solace. If a patient had an infected wound, for instance, a physician could clean it out, cover it with a bandage, and hope for the best. The patient would either heal quickly or die.

With the widespread use of antibiotics after World War II, such injuries could be treated much more effectively. Other dramatic medical advances followed quickly. By the 1960s new technologies such as improved respirators were, in the words of bioethicist Arthur Caplan, "allowing people to live when they looked dead."[1] Improvements in organ transplantation and kidney dialysis meant longer lives for people like Karen. In medical terms the revolution in health care resulting from these advances was extremely promising: doctors had many more options in treating people; infants born prematurely would no longer be condemned to death; and infectious diseases would never again, it seemed, wipe out large sections of the population.

But in social terms this revolution caused grave difficulties. The advanced forms of treatment created complex ethical dilemmas for which our legal and moral systems were unprepared. Many doctors felt they had not been trained to deal with questions such as: Should patients with a terminal or chronic illness be allowed to refuse treatment, thus hastening their own death? Should premature babies *always* be rescued, even if they face a miserable and short life?

In the late 1960s people began to think seriously about these issues and other, related ones. For instance, the abortion battle raged all over the country as states began to liberalize old statutes restricting the procedure. Journalists exposed grossly immoral scientific experiments, such as one study in the 1930s in which the U.S. Public Health Service intentionally did not treat blacks with syphilis, in order to learn about the long-term effects of the disease.

At the same time, physicians became more specialized, and patient care increasingly shifted from the doctor's office to the modern hospital. One result was that the once intimate doctor-patient relationship became strained. Medical professionals had to struggle to see that somewhere at the end of the tubes and beeping machinery that characterize high-technology care lay a person who had a family. Many patients didn't meet their doctors until they were already in the hospital and even then saw them only briefly. On top of this, the creation of Medicare and Medicaid, publicly funded health-care programs, led to increased scrutiny of doctors' practices by the press and politicians.

Patients thus became more wary of medical professionals and more willing to challenge their judgment and to sue them. The cliché "Doctor knows best"—which meant that doctors are always right and you could not question their authority—no longer applied. Practitioners had to look anew at what it meant to be a physician.

All of these changes created an interest in the young field of medical ethics, or bioethics. This discipline would not provide a "magic bullet," or surefire formula, to solve the new dilemmas. But it would give doctors, judges, and patients and their relatives a framework for sorting out the moral and legal problems confronting them.

At first, doctors turned to the ministers, priests, and rabbis who had traditionally worked alongside them, comforting the sick and the dying and providing spiritual guidance and support. Because religious leaders had always concerned themselves with moral problems, they became the first "ethicists" to work with physicians in hospitals. Now they had an active role in illuminating the moral dimensions of a problem for all the concerned parties.

By the mid-1970s doctors were calling for secular ethics experts. Drawing on concepts from such abstract fields as metaphysics, ethics, and philosophy of mind, some philosophers had begun to develop a more practical body of knowledge focusing on the moral aspects of health care and biological experimentation.

Religious leaders and philosophers joined hospital ethics committees that attempted to guide doctors in tough cases. Some of them even went on hospital rounds with doctors. But some cases were so hotly disputed they could not be contained in the medical setting. Instead they spilled over into the courts.

Decisions about life-or-death medical quandaries had previously been made by the doctor and the patient and his family, and were considered highly personal. But now the lines between life and death—lines that had once seemed clear—were being blurred by technology.

Many doctors, fearing lawsuits for medical neglect, chose to maintain life at any cost, to the dismay of some terminally ill patients who wanted an easy release from a painful existence. And patients who were permanently unconscious were being kept alive artificially by machines. Were these people "persons" in the legal and moral sense, or nothing but biologically alive tissue? Was pulling the plug murder? Because the state has an interest in the lives of its citizens, this question was often referred to judges.

In addition, legislatures became involved in medical ethics. Struggling to keep the law up to date with the new technology, they passed statutes that defined when life ends. In the early 1970s Kansas became the first state to adopt the "brain death" standard as the legal definition of death. Under this standard, people are considered dead when their entire brain has stopped functioning, even if heartbeat and breathing could be sustained by artificial life-support systems.

Webster's defines *ethics* as "the discipline dealing with what is good and bad and with moral duty and obligation." But just what is *medical ethics*? According to K. Danner Clouser, medical ethics is really no different from the ethics of everyday life.[2] The moral rules we follow in our homes, at our workplaces, and on the street—in our dealings with our friends, family, co-workers, and strangers—also apply in a medical context. "It is just that in medical ethics these familiar moral rules are being applied to situations and relationships peculiar to the medical world."

Take, for instance, the moral rule "Do not kill." This is easy enough to follow in general; few of us would violate it. But in the medical context it is a much more complicated issue. Is abortion killing? Is it killing to help someone who is terminally ill and in great pain commit suicide? Is discarding a frozen human embryo killing? That these questions and their answers are so complex is the reason medical ethics exists as a separate discipline. "It is as though it were the job of medical ethics to hold up a huge magnifying glass to the universe of medicine to see its workings more accurately," writes Clouser, "so that our standard moral rules might be applied more precisely."

Many of the ethical principles and dilemmas discussed in this book in the context of medicine come into play in your everyday life. One of the important principles is *autonomy*, your basic right to do as you please and be left alone, provided you do not interfere with the rights of others. People have claim to autonomy in all aspects of their lives, from medical care to education, to relationships with others, to political activities, to shopping.

Our country was founded largely on the basis of individual autonomy. As medical ethicist Samuel Gorovitz explains, "We who believe in the principles of liberal democracy believe not that persons exist to serve the state, but rather that political structures have their justification ultimately in the benefits that accrue to individuals.... Because we respect individuals, we subscribe to ... the Principle of Autonomy."[3]

No values are absolute, though; other principles compete with autonomy. One of these is *beneficence*, the idea that we should benefit others and take actions that will meet their needs and further their interests. When we override someone's autonomy to benefit him—do something against his wishes "for his own good"—it is called *paternalism* (or *parentalism*), as this is the way parents often act toward their children. Doctors have a special obligation to benefit their patients. The ancient Hippocratic oath taken by physicians includes the promise to "apply ... measures for the benefit of the sick according to my ability and judgment."[4]

Let's look at these competing principles in an ordinary situation: You have a friend who loves basketball. He plays in gym class even though he has a bad knee. You are worried that he is going to hurt himself seriously. You suggest that he quit, but he says he likes basketball too much and does not want to stop. Should you tell the gym teacher? If you did, you would be violating your friend's autonomy in order to benefit him.

Most likely you would decide not to notify the teacher. Our culture has a bias in favor of autonomy; generally, we do not think it right to protect people from themselves. So you would probably respect your friend's wishes, even though ultimately he might pay a high price for this.

Now let's take a more extreme situation: Your friend has been consuming a lot of alcohol. He is depressed, and you can see that his life is going to pieces. You want to help, and you start by encouraging him to give up drinking. He refuses. Should you notify someone—his parents, a teacher, a guidance counselor—of the problem? In this situation, the obligation to benefit your friend might outweigh the importance of respecting his autonomy.

What distinguishes one situation from the other and changes the equation? For one thing, the potential consequences of not acting in the second example are more troublesome: if your friend drives when he drinks, for example, he could be killed—a considerably worse fate than aggravating a bad knee. Also, the basketball player is making his decision with a clear mind. But the drinker is depressed, and his judgment is probably clouded by alcohol. His autonomy is thus already diminished.

Now we will see how the principles of autonomy and beneficence govern a medical decision. In Chapter 6 we discuss the "right to die" controversy, which raises the question of how much control a patient should have over his own care. Should a doctor respect the autonomy of a patient with a terminal illness by complying with that patient's request to discontinue treatment and let him die?

Let's take the made-up case of Susan, a patient diagnosed with terminal cancer. Chemotherapy is being used to treat the disease, but Susan requests that it be discontinued, even though this would shorten her life.

Dr. A fully respects Susan's autonomy. He believes that she is rational and that rational patients should be allowed to make these decisions themselves. It's her life, her choice. He tells her that he will not insist on more chemotherapy. Further, he will make arrangements for Susan to have nursing care at home, where she can die peacefully.

But Dr. B feels less sure. Diagnoses can be wrong—maybe with more treatment the cancer would go into remission and Susan would recover. The patient is a bit depressed—natural, given her situation, but maybe she does not really know what she wants. So Dr. B walks the fine line between persuasion and coercion: he tries to talk Susan into continuing treatment, using his authority as a doctor and warning her repeatedly that her tumor will become bigger and more painful if left untreated. Dr. B is taking a middle position on Susan's autonomy. He is questioning her right to decide for herself, yet he is not taking any legal action to force her to go on with the chemotherapy.

Dr. C is absolutely opposed to ending treatment. She believes that where there is life, there is hope, and that doctors are obligated to prolong life as much as possible. She feels a patient's autonomy does not outweigh the moral requirement that a doctor benefit her patients. Dr. C therefore goes to court to try to get Susan's wishes overruled. (In the past many doctors would have taken Dr. C's position, but now there is much greater respect for patient autonomy in the medical profession.)

Of course, the case of the alcoholic teenager and Susan's story are very different from each other. For one thing, the medical situation has variables that are far more complex. What they do share, though, is the problem of weighing the value of autonomy against that of beneficence. In approaching these dilemmas, doctors, religious thinkers, philosophers, judges, and legislators try to sort out which factors tip the scale one way or the other.

Another ethical problem that arises frequently is known as *conflicting obligations*. This refers to situations in which you owe some type of moral debt to two people whose interests clash. Satisfying your obligations to one person will mean hurting the other.

Everyone has conflicting obligations in his or her life. Let's look at a common example: You and your friend Pat have tickets to a concert Saturday night. But an hour before you are set to leave for the show, another friend, Clare, calls you. She's crying because she just had a terrible fight with her boyfriend, and they've broken up. She wants you to spend the evening at her place to cheer her up. You tell her about the concert, but she pleads with you to come over anyway, saying that she is incredibly depressed. And you remember the many times Clare has gone out of her way for you.

Even though you have been looking forward to seeing this great band, you would be happy to make the sacrifice and go comfort Clare. But what about Pat? She is counting on you also. Obviously there is no straightforward solution. You have to examine the variables and decide which course of action will be less bad.

You will consider compromises—maybe you can give the ticket to someone else; maybe you can see Clare the next day—but if none exists, you will have to decide which obligation has more importance. If you had time to poll your friends on what to do, you would probably get many different answers. An ethical dilemma is often defined in part by the fact that there is little societal agreement on how to approach it.

Doctors face conflicting obligations of perhaps a more profound nature, but the basic concept is the same for them. For instance, in Chapter 4 we discuss the controversy of "fetal rights" versus maternal rights. We raise the question of whether doctors and the courts are justified in forcing a woman to have a cesarean section against her will if that is thought necessary to ensure the health of her baby. To answer this question, doctors and judges must weigh their duty to the mother and her autonomy against their obligations to the fetus. This is a highly controversial issue, and experts have answered it in different ways.

As you read this book, try to consider the ethical problems discussed in light of your own knowledge and experience. Keep in mind that these problems, though they have scientific and technical aspects, are primarily social issues. Many have become political issues that you can influence directly. You can fight for or against abortion rights. You can vote or campaign for legislators who favor the "right to die" or for those who oppose it. You can demand that your legislators fund organ transplants, or that they instead use health-care money in ways that will help a greater number of people.

Just as you need not be a defense expert to know whether you favor increased or decreased military budgets, you need not be a doctor to take a stand on medical ethics issues. But you must have a firm grasp of the human values at stake in health care. This book is intended to help you get that grasp.

NOTES

1. Daniel Jussim, "Philosophers in Medicine," *The (Cincinnati) Enquirer Magazine*, November 7, 1982, p. 9.
2. K. Danner Clouser, "What Is Medical Ethics?" *Annals of Internal Medicine*, vol. 80, no. 5 (1974), pp. 657–660, in Richard A. Wright, *Human Values in Health Care* (New York: McGraw-Hill, 1987), pp. 273–279. Quotes are from pp. 274–5.
3. Samuel Gorovitz, *Doctors' Dilemmas* (New York: Macmillan, 1982), p. 35.
4. The Hippocratic Oath, in Richard A. Wright, *Human Values in Health Care* (New York: McGraw-Hill, 1987), p. 283.

ADDITIONAL SOURCES

Daniel Callahan, "Contemporary Medical Ethics," *New England Journal of Medicine*, May 29, 1980, pp. 1228–1233.

"Do You Still Know What's Ethical?" *Medical Economics*, April 3, 1989, pp. 2–10.

Deborah Franklin, "The Theologian," *Hippocrates*, May/June 1988, pp. 84–91.

Russ Rymer, "The Judge," *Hippocrates*, May/June 1988, pp. 54–62.

CHAPTER TWO

ABORTION AND TEENAGERS

MEDICAL care for teenagers presents some unique ethical problems. Many of these arise because of uncertainties over how grown up they are. Some adolescents are actually more mature than some adults. Should they have the same right as adults do to make medical treatment decisions for themselves?

In general, they do not have this right. Although many people agree that a young person should make a significant contribution to such decisions, as a group teenagers are not considered mature enough to make them without their parents' help. There are, however, exceptions to this in the law, particularly in the areas of contraception and abortion.

When teens' power is limited, do parents always have the ultimate say in their treatment decisions? Not necessarily. In some cases, if society does not approve of a decision parents

ABORTION AND TEENAGERS

make for their severely ill teenager, it will intervene through the judicial system and impose *its* judgments on the family. This may happen even if the young patient agrees with his or her parents' decision.

In the next two chapters we will examine the relationship between adolescents and their parents, and between the state and the family, when a medical decision needs to be made for a teenager. These relationships are complex and may be loaded with conflict, and that makes it all the more important for you to understand them. The knowledge will allow you to better control your own medical care and to understand why you may not have complete control in this area until you have reached adulthood.

TEEN PREGNANCY

"*July 1985*

"*To Whom It May Concern:*
"*When I was 14, I ran away from home as my father was a drunkard and beat my mother and I, too often.*

"*I could set type, so I found a job at night in a little town some fifty miles away.*

"*One night the editor of the paper decided to rape me. I fought like a maniac and he knocked me down. I hit my head and went out like a light. When I cam[e] to I was in an alley!*

"*In about two months, I knew he'd done this dastardly deed and I was pregnant. I went to the town doctor but he wouldn't DARE help me. He told me, though, that at 4 months one could cause a miscarriage quite easily and safely with a catheter.*

"*Well, I was between the devil and deep sea. I told the editor what he'd done and threatened to tell his wife. But I need the job and I sure couldn't go home. He just laughed and said no one would believe me. I kep[t] myself there and used the catheter at 4 mos. Was scared but got through it O.K. and saved myself a lot of gossip, thank God. I managed to get a good job up in Illinois and no one ever knew of my horrible experience. I would never have wanted a baby born under such circumstances.**

In most states in this country, children become adults, for legal purposes, at age eighteen. Once you reach that age, you are presumed by law to be competent to make medical decisions for yourself. Before that age, you are presumed to be legally incompetent, and health-care workers are likely to require your parents' consent for most medical procedures. There are exceptions to this: "emancipated" minors—those who have married, for instance—are treated as adults. Also, many states have laws allowing all minors to be diagnosed and treated without parental consent for sexually transmitted diseases (STD's) or substance abuse.

According to law professor Alexander Morgan Capron, these laws are passed for practical reasons, not in recognition of teens' rights to control their own lives. Authorities realize that teens will be more likely to get treatment for embarrassing medical problems if they are afforded confidentiality.[1]

Only because these problems cause social ills and can have severe consequences for the individual do authorities grant this confidentiality. If you are a teenager, the extent of your medical rights in a given situation depends partly on whether you have a "social disease" or merely a personal one. The increase of problems like drug and alcohol abuse and STD's among teens has given them more power to make medical choices without their parents' consent.

Another social problem involving such choices is teen pregnancy. This territory is hotly contested. Some people believe that teens should have the same free access to birth control and contraception as they do to drug rehabilitation programs. Others disagree, arguing that teenagers are not ready to be treated as adults in this area. Teen sexual activity often creates intense conflict between parents and children. Now this conflict has spread outside of that relationship, to society as a whole, as the

*From a letter sent to the National Abortion Rights Action League.

ABORTION AND TEENAGERS

community tries to decide if teens' access to birth control and abortion should be restricted.

It has been estimated that 70 percent of all girls and 80 percent of boys engage in sexual intercourse as teenagers. Because teens are not likely to use birth control regularly and are more fertile now than at any other time in their lives, pregnancies occur often. Every year, more than 1 million teenage girls in the United States become pregnant. Ninety-two percent of these pregnancies are unintended (excluding pregnancies among married teens), and almost half end in abortion. Almost one in five women in this country will have had an abortion before turning twenty. And more than one-fourth of all U.S. abortions are performed on teens.

Many young teens who do have babies put themselves at serious risk by failing to get sufficient medical attention during the pregnancy. This means they are much more likely than older teens or adults to have health problems related to being pregnant and to give birth to premature babies, or babies with low birth weight, who may not be healthy. When they become parents, teenagers often end up on welfare; only one in fifty graduates from college.

What should be done about the problem of teenage pregnancy? On this issue people with conservative social views differ strongly from those with liberal ones:

- Conservatives favor a return to "traditional values," including tight parental control over children; they resent laws permitting their children to get medical treatment without their permission. Liberals believe that children can make many of their own decisions and that sometimes they have to be protected from their parents.

- Conservatives encourage abstinence from premarital sex; liberals encourage sex education, so teen sex will not result in pregnancy.

- Conservatives want to see restrictions on access to contraception and abortion; liberals campaign for free access.

The United States Supreme Court has played a key role in determining where the line will be drawn in some of these conflicts. The Court's 1965 decision in *Griswold v. Connecticut* established for the first time that citizens have a constitutional right to privacy; the Court struck down a Connecticut law barring anyone from prescribing contraceptives to married adults. In 1977 the Supreme Court case *Carey v. Population Services International* extended to minors the right to have access to contraceptives.

The landmark *Roe v. Wade* case was decided by the Supreme Court in 1973. It gave women across the country the right to choose abortion. (The abortion issue in general is discussed in Chapter 4.) In the aftermath of *Roe*, many attempts have been made to restrict teens' access to abortion by involving parents in the abortion decision.

PARENTAL-INVOLVEMENT LAWS

Thirty-two states in the country have laws mandating parents' involvement in abortion decisions. The stated purpose of these laws is to protect the well-being of teenagers by encouraging them to discuss with their parents whether or not to get an abortion. By involving their parents, teens get emotional support and help in making a rational decision. Parents may have information about their daughter's medical history that she does not know about. And they can play a valuable role in her medical and psychological care following the abortion.

In addition to serving the child's interest in these ways, the laws also support parental authority. For example, parents whose religious beliefs do not condone abortion may want to express this to their daughter or forbid her outright to terminate the pregnancy. Parental-involvement laws improve the chances that they will be able to do so.

Some supporters of parental-involvement laws think these restrictions will decrease teen pregnancy. Their logic is that

Demonstrators in front of the Supreme Court express opinions on both sides of the abortion question.

when teenagers face barriers to abortion, they will be more careful about birth control or will abstain from sex.

There is also a belief that the laws will deter minors from getting abortions and encourage them instead to carry their pregnancies to term. In this the statutes appear successful. Parental-involvement laws do decrease the number of abortions teenagers have.

Those who advocate abortion rights believe this decrease results from the laws' creating a tremendous obstacle to young women exercising their freedom of choice. Anti-abortion forces, on the other hand, claim that with her parents' support, a teenager is more likely to carry the child to term. Whatever the reason, between 1981 and 1984 the birth rate for teens fifteen to seventeen years old in Minneapolis increased by 35.8 percent. A representative of the Minneapolis Health Department said this was a result of the parental-involvement law there.

According to studies, 50 to 65 percent of teenagers, of their own free will, reveal their pregnancies to their mother, their father, or both. Younger teens tell their parents more often than older ones. The American Civil Liberties Union, which supports abortion rights and is opposed to parental-involvement laws, argues that those who do not want to tell their parents have good reasons. They may, for instance, fear further damaging relationships in a family already filled with problems and conflicts.[2]

Minnesota Citizens Concerned for Life (MCCL), an anti-abortion group, agrees that many teens are reluctant to notify their parents, but feels this reluctance is usually the result of exaggerated fears. Teens may find it difficult to discuss a sex-related problem with their parents; may fear that parents will be angry, disappointed, or ashamed of them; and are more likely to consult their friends than their parents when making a decision. MCCL believes that since parents will actually be supportive in most cases, parental-involvement statutes can facilitate family communication.[3]

HODGSON V. MINNESOTA

A Supreme Court ruling in July 1989, *Webster v. Reproductive Health Services*, allowed states to restrict abortions for all women in new ways. Since then much of the attention in the abortion issue has focused on the privacy rights of minors. While the public seems reluctant to impose new restrictions on abortion for adult women, a large majority—70 percent, according to a September 1989 *New York Times*/CBS News poll—favors parental-involvement laws. The Supreme Court has ruled on two

ABORTION AND TEENAGERS

cases involving parental-involvement laws—one from Ohio, the other from Minnesota.

The Minnesota case was initiated in 1981 by a group of individuals, represented by the American Civil Liberties Union (ACLU), who filed a class action suit, *Hodgson v. Minnesota*, challenging the constitutionality of a parental-involvement law about to go into effect in the state. The law said that before performing an abortion on an unmarried woman under eighteen, a doctor must notify both of her parents. Even if they are divorced and the second parent is not at all involved with the child, he or she must still be notified. Alternatively, a minor who does not want to tell a parent can appear before a state judge in a "bypass procedure" and request a court order allowing the abortion. If she could convince a state judge that she was sufficiently mature or that telling her parents was not in her best interest, the requirement would be waived.

A trial was held in a U.S. district court in Minnesota.[4] The testimony established that:

- Half of the teens in Minnesota live in single-parent homes. If they become pregnant, many voluntarily notify the parent living with them. But unless they are willing to go to court for the bypass procedure, they must also tell the other parent—even if that person is playing no role in their life. This can result in the second parent's returning to the family in a disruptive way at a time when everyone else is under great stress.

- The battering of women by their male partners may be the most often committed violent crime in Minnesota. Many minors are also victims of family abuse including rape, incest, neglect, and beatings. Notifying an abusive father of the pregnancy can provoke violence against the daughter or mother.

- Going through the judicial bypass procedure can be traumatic; sometimes it is more troublesome than the abortion operation itself. Many minors are fearful of the judge and resent having to justify their decision and give personal information to a total stranger. One teen said, "the thought of people who I didn't know, who I had never seen before, asking me questions about my personal life, wondering what I was. . . It was scary."[5]

The state did not convince district court judge Donald D. Alsop that the law protects pregnant teens or promotes family communication or better family relations. Since the law deprived minors of their constitutional right to abortion and did not serve a state interest, Alsop ruled it unconstitutional.

But by the time the case was decided on appeal by the U.S. Supreme Court,[6] the high court no longer considered abortion a basic constitutional right. A five-to-four majority agreed that laws requiring notice to both parents "resulted in major trauma to the child, and often a parent as well." The Court decided, however, that as long as such laws contain a judicial bypass procedure for avoiding two-parent notification, they are acceptable. The Court also upheld Ohio's statute, which requires notice to only one parent.

As we have seen, decisions involving abortion for a teenager sometimes create conflict between the child and her parents. Parents may turn to the state for help in upholding their authority, making the government their ally. The teenager may be opposed to the actions of both parties, even if sometimes those actions will benefit her.

In the next chapter we will look at situations in which the teen is more likely to be in agreement with her parents. In caring for the adolescent with a severe illness, the conflict may instead be between the state and the whole family. The state may impose its judgments on the parents and the teen, believing that it is acting in the teen's best interest. The family may object to this, even though ultimately it may benefit the teen.

NOTES

1. Alexander Morgan Capron, "The Competence of Children as Self-Deciders in Biomedical Interventions," in Willard Gaylin and Ruth Macklin, eds., *Who Speaks for the Child?* (New York: Plenum, 1982), pp. 59–60.
2. Janet Benshoof, et al., "Parental Notice Laws" (pamphlet; New York: American Civil Liberties Union Reproductive Freedom Project, 1986), pp. 5–6.
3. Minnesota Citizens Concerned for Life, Brief Amicus Curiae in Support of the State of Minnesota in the U.S. Court of Appeals for the Eighth Circuit (friend of the court brief in *Hodgson v. Minnesota*), not dated, p. 5.
4. *Hodgson v. Minnesota*, 648 Federal Supplement 756 (District Court of Minnesota, 1986).
5. Deposition of Elizabeth S., quoted in Janet Benshoof, et al., "Parental Notice Laws," p. 13.
6. Linda Greenhouse, "States May Require Girl to Notify Parents Before Having Abortion," *The New York Times*, June 26, 1990, pp. A1, A20; and "Excerpts from Court's Ruling on Minnesota's Abortion Law," *The New York Times*, June 26, 1990, p. A20.

ADDITIONAL SOURCES

R.W. Apple, Jr., "Limits on Abortion Seem Less Likely," *The New York Times*, September 29, 1989, p. A13.

Carey v. Population Services International, 431 U.S. 678 (1977).

Linda Greenhouse, "Abortion Law Fight Turns to Rights of Teen-Agers," *The New York Times*, July 16, 1989, pp. 1, 23.

Jane Hodgson, et al., Petition for a Writ of Certiori to the United States Court of Appeals for the Eighth Circuit (petition to the U.S. Supreme Court to hear the case *Hodgson v. Minnesota*), January 5, 1989.

Angela Holder, *Legal Issues in Pediatrics and Adolescent Medicine*, 2d ed. (New Haven, Conn.: Yale University Press, 1985).

Robert Mnookin, *In the Interest of Children* (New York: W. H. Freeman, 1985).

Eva Rubin, *The Supreme Court and the American Family* (New York: Greenwood Press, 1986).

ORGANIZATIONS

The following organizations provided some of the materials for this chapter. Contact them for further information.

In favor of parental-involvement laws:

Minnesota Citizens Concerned for Life
4249 Nicollet Ave. S
Minneapolis, MN 55409

National Right to Life
Suite 500
419 Seventh St. NW
Washington, DC 20004-2293

Opposed to parental-involvement laws:

American Civil Liberties Union
132 W. 43rd St.
New York, NY 10036

National Abortion Rights Action League
1101 Fourteenth St. NW
Fifth floor
Washington, DC 20005

CHAPTER THREE

WHO SPEAKS FOR THE TEENAGER?

EVERYONE knows that being ill is an awful experience in itself. For teens it may be particularly hard; youth is usually a time of good health and high energy, and young people tend to think of themselves as invincible and immortal. It is even more difficult when a sick teen has to cope also with ethical questions about his or her medical care.

TEENAGERS' LIVES ON THE LINE

Karen was sixteen years old when her kidneys failed. After unsuccessfully transplanting one of her father's kidneys into Karen, doctors put her on dialysis, a process in which a machine does the work the kidneys are supposed to do: blood is removed through an artery, toxins are filtered out, and the purified blood is returned through a vein. She suffered many unpleasant side effects from the procedure, including chills, nausea, vomiting, bad headaches, and weakness. In an article, her doctors described her case:

"After it was clear that the kidney would never function, Karen and her parents expressed the wish to stop medical treatment and let 'nature takes its course.' ... Staff members conveyed to the family that such wishes were unheard of and unacceptable, and that a decision to stop treatment could never be an alternative. The family did decide to continue dialysis, medication, and diet therapy. Karen's renal [kidney] incapacity returned to pretransplant levels and she returned to a socially isolated life, diet restriction, chronic discomfort, and fatigue.

"[In May] Karen, with her parents' agreement, refused ... any further dialysis.

"Karen died on June 2, with both parents at her bedside. ... Shortly [before] her death she thanked the staff for what she knew had been a hard time for them and she told her parents she hoped they would be happy. We later learned that before her death she had written a will and picked a burial spot near her home and near her favorite horseback riding trail. In the final days she supported her parents as they faltered in their decision; she told her father, 'Daddy, I will be happy there [in the ground] if there is no machine and they don't work on me any more.'"*

Society has a special interest in protecting children, and that makes cases like Karen's especially difficult. Had Karen been an adult, the doctors would not have been as reluctant to follow her wishes and stop treatment. But Karen was a minor, and this gave them pause. Children are generally considered more weak, dependent, and vulnerable than adults, and somewhat less able to make decisions for themselves.

In cases where children are immature, parents are generally allowed to make decisions for them. This is because it is

---

*From John E. Schowalter, et al., "The Adolescent Patient's Decision to Die," *Pediatrics*, January 1973, p. 98.

assumed that parents love their kids, know them better than anyone else, and will act to further their children's best interests. Also, a long tradition recognizes the rights of parents to raise their children as they see fit, imparting those values they deem appropriate. If they harm their children, however—by abuse or neglect, which can include refusing medical care for them—society will take steps to rescue the children.

Drawing the line between parents' and children's rights on the one hand and society's interest in protecting children on the other is one of the most difficult problems in medical ethics. In this chapter we will examine this problem in cases involving adolescents.

Karen was mature, and although she had her parents' support, she was the chief decision-maker regarding her care. Karen's doctors at first wanted to "rescue" her by overriding her wishes and those of her parents. Karen was, after all, not terminally but chronically ill—the dialysis could have prolonged her life indefinitely. But they came to recognize that dialysis caused her great pain and discomfort, it offered little chance of improving her condition, and therefore, she rationally preferred the only alternative: death.

Two doctors and a social worker who had helped to treat Karen explained that "older adolescents, like our patient, can appreciate their suffering and fatigue and can comprehend when it is likely that life will never offer any more than continued disability, doubt, and suffering."[1] The hospital decided not to seek a court order forcing her to continue with the procedure.

Children did not always have the right to influence or determine their own destiny, nor has the state always taken an interest in protecting them. At one time, parents had free rein. In colonial America children were treated very much as if they were the property of their parents. Parents could require that they turn over their wages and be absolutely obedient. In Massachusetts in the 1600s a child over sixteen years old could be executed for hitting his parents or guardians.

This state of affairs was a result of conditions that are foreign to most Americans today. For one thing, the whole family

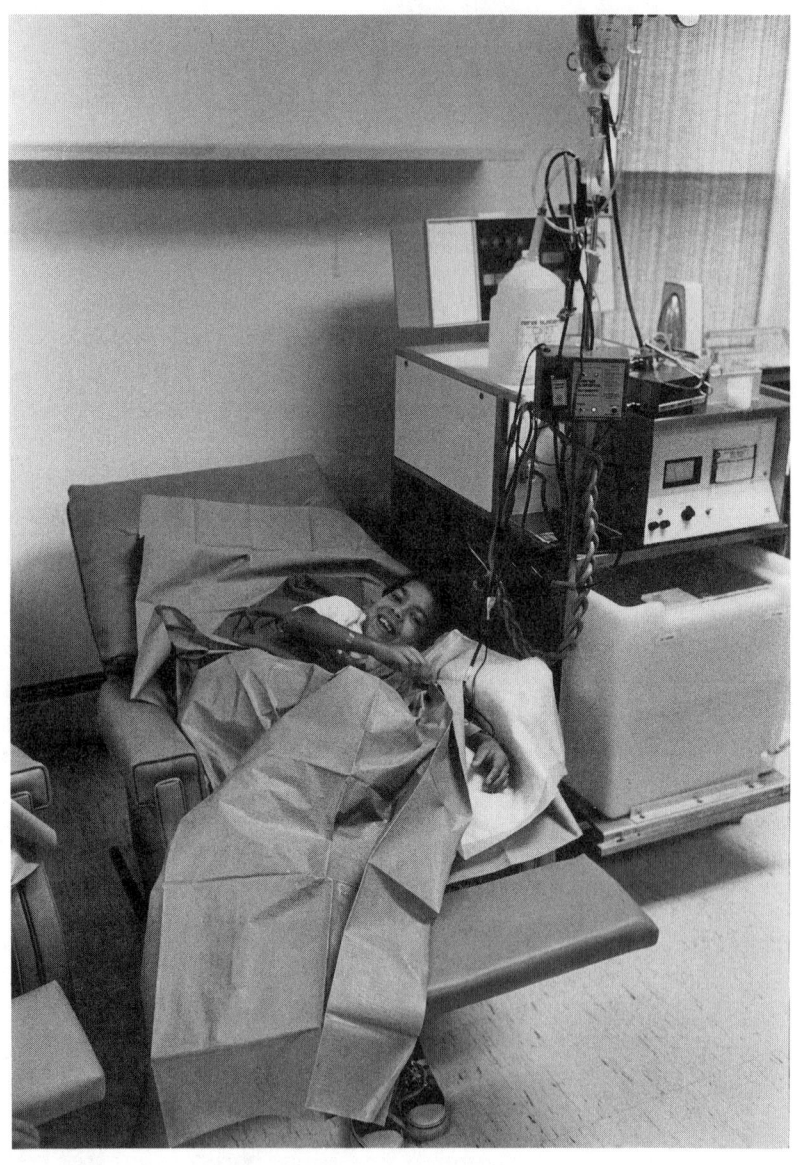

Young people with kidney disease must depend on dialysis machines to keep them alive.

needed to work or they would perish. For another, the rigid morality of the Puritans required parents to keep their offspring under tight control. The goal was for children to be well behaved so they could ultimately achieve religious salvation.

During the nineteenth century this system of parental control started to diminish. Adults began to recognize that childhood was a special time, distinct from later years, and that children needed to be nurtured emotionally. The brutal exploitation of child laborers began to horrify many people; at the same time, there was increasing demand for workers with greater skills.

To deal with the new circumstances the government initiated compulsory education, passed laws limiting children's role in the work force, and created child welfare laws. Now parents could no longer use their children primarily as a source of income. And if they abused or neglected their offspring, the state would intervene and take the children away.

The next big change took place in the late 1960s, when children started to claim some constitutional rights. In a landmark case the Supreme Court ruled that children accused of delinquency were entitled to protections in court similar to those enjoyed by adult defendants. The Court also found that children have free speech rights. Later decisions gave minors rights to contraception and abortion, as we discussed in Chapter 2.

That children have greater protections and more rights may represent an advance for our society, but it has also made the relationship between the state and the family much more complex. In the past, parents would have made a decision for a sick child like Karen and no one would have questioned it. Now courts, doctors, or hospital ethics committees may try to overrule the parents, and the child must also be heard from.

This has made it necessary to develop criteria as to when children are mature enough to play a part in medical decisions. According to Thomas and Celia Scully, a child is able to give informed consent for his treatment when he can:

- *understand* the situation because he has intelligence, can form concepts, and has knowledge about his illness

- *reason*—that is, think and express himself logically and rationally

- *communicate* clearly so others can understand him

Before child-labor laws were passed, children worked long hours in factories and mills.

- *volunteer*—make independent judgments regarding what is right for him without being coerced by authority figures such as doctors and parents.[2]

The extent to which children of different ages can contribute to decisions about their care varies with the individual involved. While most children do not meet all four of these criteria before age fourteen, many younger than that can give their informed *assent* to medical care. That is, though they do not have full decision-making power, they can express their desires about care and have adults give these desires serious consideration. In studies of children with cancer, for instance, patients as young as six were able to participate in treatment decisions.

It has also been necessary to develop criteria as to when the state may intervene in family affairs. Generally, if it is unclear whether or not a certain treatment is in a child's best interest, as in Karen's case, the family can refuse it. If, on the other hand, it is certain that a medical procedure is necessary to save the child's life and that that life will be worth living, the family cannot refuse.

Many cases involve parents who have tried to refuse their children lifesaving treatment that violated their religious beliefs. For instance, Jehovah's Witnesses have refused blood transfusions for their children. The Witnesses are a Christian sect whose religious beliefs, based on Bible passages prohibiting the eating of blood, do not allow them to receive transfusions. According to their religion, those who accept transfusions will be damned for eternity in the afterlife. Given this belief, it is easy to see why Witnesses think their children would be better off dying—and losing the relatively short time left to them as mortals—than receiving a blood transfusion and suffering damnation forever. Society as a whole, however, does not share this belief.

The 1974 Jehovah's Witnesses case *In re Pogue*[3] illustrates well the difference between adults' rights to make medical choices for themselves and to make identical choices for their children. A mother and her baby needed blood transfusions or they would die; the mother refused the transfusions for herself and her child. A District of Columbia superior court accepted the mother's refusal for herself, but ordered treatment for the baby.

The reasoning was that giving an adult blood transfusions against her wishes, even in a case where the alternative was death, would violate her constitutionally protected rights to practice her religion and determine her own medical care. She could not, however, sacrifice her child in pursuit of these rights.

Another important precedent in this area, *Jehovah's Witnesses of Washington v. King County Hospital*,[4] was decided in 1967 by a federal district court and later upheld by the U.S. Supreme Court. A group of Jehovah's Witnesses whose children had been given court-ordered blood transfusions brought the case as a class action on behalf of the 8,900 Witnesses in the state of Washington.

They challenged a law under which their children had been placed in the legal protection of a court so that a transfusion could be given. This occurred even though they had provided doctors and hospitals with a document releasing them from liability and had also consented to any necessary treatment that did not involve transfusion. They contended that the law violated their freedom of religion, their right of family privacy, and other constitutional rights.

In rejecting the Witnesses' arguments, the court cited a Supreme Court decision in a case not involving medicine but sharing an important principle. In *Prince v. Massachusetts* the aunt and guardian of a nine-year-old girl encouraged her to sell Bible tracts on the streets, in violation of the Massachusetts child labor laws. The woman argued that the child was exercising her constitutional right to freedom of religion. But the Court didn't agree, finding that:

> neither rights of religion nor rights of parenthood are beyond limitation. Acting to guard the general interest in youth's well being, the state ... may restrict the parent's control by ... regulating or prohibiting the child's labor, and in many other ways. Its authority is not nullified merely because the parent grounds his claim to control the child's course of conduct on religion or conscience.... Parents may be free to become martyrs themselves. But it does not follow they are free ... to make martyrs of their children.[5]

In cases in which clearly beneficial lifesaving treatment is available to an endangered child, it is usually concluded that such treatment is in the child's best interest. Courts have considered the state's interest in the child's life more important than the parents' beliefs—religious or otherwise, and even if the child shares the beliefs—and have granted physicians court orders to operate.

But when the outcome of the treatment is in doubt—for instance, in combatting certain childhood cancers—a trickier issue is raised. Here, vetoing a family's decision not to treat does not necessarily benefit the child, but might hurt the parent-child relationship as well as the relationship between the family and the physicians. Some doctors feel that in these circumstances the family's wishes should be honored. The story of Karen illustrates the dilemma.

Although Karen and her parents did not base their decision on religious belief, their situation raised some of the same issues as the Jehovah's Witnesses case. Just as the Jehovah's Witnesses' children risked death if transfusions were denied them, Karen would die if treatment was stopped. The big difference for Karen, though, was that dialysis made her feel awful, and there was little chance that her condition would improve. Blood transfusions, on the other hand, are not a lifelong physical burden, and they are often performed in cases in which the patient has excellent prospects for recovery.

Sometimes the conflict between the family and society is caused not by religious beliefs, but by a disagreement between parents and doctors over how to best help a sick child. This happened in the case of a different Karen—a twelve-year-old girl diagnosed with Hodgkin's disease, which causes anemia and swelling of vital organs.[6] Doctors wanted to treat the disease in a conventional way, using surgery and chemotherapy. This would give Karen a 90 percent chance of living at least five more years. Without treatment she would probably live two years at most.

Karen's parents wanted to spare their daughter the side effects of this therapy, and took her to a foreign clinic that tried to combat the disease in a less intrusive way—using nutritional therapy and herbs. But when they returned to the United States, officials removed her from her class at school, put her in foster care for three days, and didn't let her talk to her parents. A judge ordered a medical examination, and doctors concluded that conventional treatment would be best for Karen. The parents still refused, pleading to be allowed to do what they thought best for their daughter. The case made headlines, and many people were upset over what they saw as a violation of the parents' rights.

The case ended up in federal district court, where Judge Richard Minor returned Karen to her parents. He told them, "You are facing an awesome decision to subject Karen to the unpleasant, painful, and possibly crippling effects of radiation and chemotherapy... or you may see her die. I would advise you to let your doctor tell you when the time has come... to change treatment to keep Karen alive. I certainly tell you that I am not qualified to make that decision and frankly, I don't think you are either." The parents didn't follow his advice, and Karen died less than a year and a half later.

Authors Thomas and Celia Scully criticize the handling of this case. They point out that Judge Minor refused to let Karen speak for herself. It is possible, they argue, that she was mature enough to participate in crucial medical decisions. Karen's lawyer asked Judge Minor to let her testify, but the judge said he was "most reluctant to subject a twelve-year-old to the trauma." The Scullys also believe that the furor over the "kidnapping" of Karen interfered with rational decison-making; seen in perspective, "the medical evidence would have tipped the balance in favor of ordering conventional treatment."

NON-LIFE-THREATENING CASES

So far we have considered cases in which a teenager's life hinged on a treatment decison. But what about situations in which a teenager whose life is not threatened could possibly be *helped* in some way by medical care? By looking at three such cases, we will see that decisions here can be equally agonizing.

The 1955 case *In re Seiferth*[7] involved Martin Seiferth, Jr., a fourteen-year-old living in upstate New York. He had been born with a cleft palate (a divide in the roof of the mouth) and a harelip (the upper lip is split, like that of a hare). As a result, his face was disfigured and he could not speak normally.

Neither the boy nor his father would consent to surgery to correct the condition. The father believed in mental healing, letting "the forces of the universe work on the body." He said this was not a religious belief. He was not opposed to surgery if that's what Martin wanted. But under his father's influence, Martin had come to believe in mental healing himself, and said he wanted to wait a while longer before undergoing surgery.

The boy had good grades—all over 90 the last school year—and he had a newspaper route. His father testified that his son had lately withdrawn a bit from his peers, but "As soon as anyone contacts Martin, he is so likable nobody is tempted to ridicule him. ... Through his pleasantness he overcomes it."

Officials at the Erie County Health Department went to court to have the boy declared "neglected" and to assume temporary custody so they could force him to undergo low-risk surgery to repair the harelip and cleft palate. A plastic surgeon testified that adolescence "is an extremely important period" for someone to be able to look and speak normally.

He said that children with Martin's condition are almost always operated on earlier in life—usually at one to three years of age—with speech training beginning in grade school or earlier. Further, the longer Martin waited, the less effective surgery would become and the less available speech-training facilities would be. However, he acknowledged that the condition was not an emergency and that surgery could be performed at any time.

The Court of Appeals of New York ruled that Martin did not have to undergo surgery. The decision was based on the fact that successful treatment of the boy required intensive speech therapy, which was impossible without Martin's cooperation. The plastic surgeon "did not attempt to view the case from the psychological viewpoint of this misguided youth," according to the ruling; since Martin did not want surgery and would object to undergoing speech therapy afterward, he would not benefit from an operation.

But the dissenting judges saw it differently, believing that Martin's "chance for a normal, useful life" was threatened by his not having surgery: "What these parents are doing, by their failure to provide for an operation, however well-intentioned, is far worse than beating the child or denying him food or clothing. ... Normalcy and happiness ... will unquestionably be impossible if the disfigurement is not corrected." Just because a parent has his child's approval for neglecting him doesn't make the neglect permissible, argued the dissenters.

Postscript: When Martin was older, he decided he didn't want the surgery. He went to a vocational high school where he learned the upholstery trade, graduated at the head of his class, went into business for himself, and was successful. The Erie County Health Department did not change its position on the case, believing the operation would have given Martin "a fuller opportunity for the development of his talents."[8]

In the *Seiferth* case the court ruled against forced surgery because it would not be in the child's best interest. The dissent felt that it would be. But neither side mentioned whether the child or the father had a specific right to refuse the surgery. By the reasoning of both opinions, under other circumstances the court could have ordered the surgery over the family's wishes. This is what occurred in the case *In re Sampson*,[9] which was heard before the same court fifteen years later.

Fifteen-year-old Kevin Sampson had Von Recklinghausen's disease, which resulted in, as a judge put it, "a large fold of overgrowth of tissue causing the right eyelid, cheek, corner of the mouth and ear to droop badly." While the disease had no cure, it did not threaten Kevin's life. Because of his disfigurement, however, he had been exempted from school for six years and was virtually illiterate. A psychologist found him to be extremely dependent and to have feelings of inferiority.

The Ulster County commissioner of health brought a neglect proceeding, saying that Kevin's mother should have her son operated on for his condition. The surgery that could improve the function and appearance of the boy's face would require blood transfusions and was risky. One surgeon said, "I think it's a dangerous procedure.... It's a massive surgery of six to eight hours duration with great blood loss."

Kevin's only living parent, his mother, was a Jehovah's Witness; she would not agree to surgery if transfusions were involved. The surgeon recommended waiting until Kevin was 21 (the age of legal majority at the time), when he could decide for himself. The operation would also be less risky then. However, the court ordered the surgery, ruling that this wait would be too costly: "If this boy has any chance at all for a normal, happy existence, without a disfigurement so gross as to overshadow all else in his life, some risk must be taken." The court also found the state's interest in the child's health of greater importance than the mother's religious beliefs.

In *Sampson* the state took over the role traditionally played by parents, while in *Seiferth* the court implied that such state action is acceptable. Law professor Joseph Goldstein objects to interference with parental autonomy in these types of cases because it ignores "each child's biological and psychological need for unthreatened and unbroken continuity of care by his parents." Noting the difficulty in assessing the risks and the benefits of treatment or nontreatment, he asks, "How can parents in such situations give the wrong answer since there is no way of knowing the right answer?"[10]

Some courts have strongly favored the right of the parents to decide. In 1972 the Supreme Court of Pennsylvania ruled *In re Ricky Ricardo Green*[11] that the state's interest does not outweigh a parent's religious beliefs in cases in which "the child's life is *not immediately imperiled* by his physical condition."

Ricky was sixteen and had suffered from polio, which caused obesity and curvature of the spine. He could not stand or walk. The dangerous operation that could correct this condition, "spinal fusion," would involve transferring bone from the pelvis to the spine. The court recognized that the operation would be beneficial, but it would not be necessary to save Ricky's life.

The procedure would require blood transfusions; Ricky's mother, a Jehovah's Witness, would not consent. (His parents were separated.)

In its decision the court cited a Supreme Court ruling that exempted Amish children from compulsory education, on the grounds that education past a certain age violated their families' religious practices. By the same logic, Jehovah's Witnesses children shouldn't be subject to unnecessary surgery that would go against *their* families' religion.

The court also considered Ricky's feelings about the operation. He was opposed to the surgery both on religious grounds and because he had already been hospitalized for a long period and no one "says [the operation] is going to come out right." In finding out Ricky's wishes before ruling, the Pennsylvania court recognized the right of a mature and intelligent teenager to have a say in his own health care. This is the same right doctors honored in the case of Karen, the girl with kidney failure whose story started off this chapter.

In the last two chapters we have looked at ethical issues unique to the medical care of teenagers. Problems occur here because society does not consider teens to be as mature as adults, yet it recognizes them as being more mature than young children. Therefore, their ability to make medical decisions, their parents' power over them, and the role of the state are in a gray area. Such murky issues in medical ethics are those most likely to lead to uncertainty, misunderstanding, and conflict.

The rest of this book deals with more general issues that affect people of all ages. Reproduction, care for the critically ill, transplants—these and other issues may play a role in anyone's life. Even if they are not directly involved in yours right now, chances are they will affect a family member. Besides, controversies in these areas will influence our evolving values, and these values affect not just our medical care, but everything we do. This makes it crucial for all citizens to understand them.

NOTES

1. John E. Schowalter et al., "The Adolescent Patient's Decision to Die," *Pediatrics*, January 1973, p. 99.
2. Thomas Scully and Celia Scully, *Making Medical Decisions* (New York: Simon & Schuster, 1987), pp. 254–56.
3. Court case discussed in Thomas Scully and Celia Scully, *Making Medical Decisions*, p. 247.
4. *Jehovah's Witnesses of Washington* v. *King County Hospital*, 278 Federal Supplement 488.
5. Quoted in *Jehovah's Witnesses* v. *King County Hospital*, p. 504.
6. Case discussed in Thomas Scully and Celia Scully, *Making Medical Decisions*, pp. 230–32, 250–51. Quotes are from pp. 232, 251.
7. *In re Seiferth*, 309 NY 80, 127 NE 2D 820 (NY 1955). Quotes are from 309 NY 80, pp. 80, 84, 85, 87.
8. Letter from the county attorney of Erie County to Joseph Goldstein, quoted in Joseph Goldstein, "Medical Care for the Child at Risk," in Willard Gaylin and Ruth Macklin, eds., *Who Speaks for the Child?* (New York: Plenum, 1982), p. 184.
9. *In re Sampson*, 328 NYS 2D 686 (NY 1972), 323 NYS 2D 253 (NY 1971), 317 NYS 2D 641 (Family Court, 1970). Quotes are from 323 NYS 2D 253, p. 254; 317 NYS 2D 641, pp. 645, 657.
10. Joseph Goldstein, "Medical Care for the Child at Risk," in Willard Gaylin and Ruth Macklin, eds., *Who Speaks for the Child?* (New York: Plenum, 1982). Quotes are from pp. 159, 166.
11. *In re Green*, 452 Pa. 373, 307 A.2D 279 (Pa. 1972); 292 A.2D 387 (Pa. 1972). Quotes are from 292 A.2D 387, p. 392; 307 A.2D 279, p. 280.

ADDITIONAL SOURCES

Adrienne Asch, et al., "Who Should Decide?" *Hastings Center Report*, December 1987, pp. 17–21.

Ruth Macklin, *Mortal Choices* (Boston: Houghton Mifflin, 1987).

James Morrissey, et al., *Consent and Confidentiality in the Health Care of Children* (New York: The Free Press, 1986).

Margaret O'Brien Steinfels, "Children's Rights, Parental Rights, Family Privacy, and Family Autonomy," in Willard Gaylin and Ruth Macklin, eds., *Who Speaks for the Child?* (New York: Plenum, 1982).

CHAPTER FOUR

REPRODUCTION

No subject in medical ethics affects as many people and is as controversial as human reproduction. The confrontations between anti-abortion protesters and abortion rights activists in front of abortion clinics are frequent reminders of how much this issue has divided our society. The growing number of babies born to drug-using mothers raises urgent questions over how this trend can be reversed and whether it justifies state intrusion into women's lives. New reproductive technologies offer a "brave new world" of test-tube babies and threaten to alter the structure of the family.

Many of these problems do not easily lend themselves to compromise; they involve a clash in basic values. For instance, in the abortion debate people who believe human life begins when a sperm fertilizes an egg are inclined to see the mother's

REPRODUCTION

autonomy as irrelevant. Those who argue that the mother's right to control her own body is all important tend to ignore the fetus.

You may already have strong beliefs on some of these issues. But the fact that they are so emotional and divisive makes it all the more important to understand the opposing arguments, to question your own beliefs, and to see those who disagree with you not as enemies but as people with a different, and perhaps equally valid, perspective.

ABORTION

Abortion can be many things—a simple medical procedure; a difficult personal decision; a social and political conflict dividing the nation. On each of these levels it poses an ethical dilemma: the life of the fetus is pitted against the needs or desires—or occasionally the life—of the mother.

Each year 1.6 million abortions are performed in the United States. The high frequency of abortion is a result of the many unintended pregnancies that occur here. Many people fail to use birth control, and contraceptives often fail when they are employed.

Most abortions take place in the first twelve weeks of pregnancy, and are achieved by a technique called "suction curettage," in which the contents of the uterus are removed by vacuum. The procedure is safe—much safer than childbirth, in fact—and can be performed in a clinic or doctor's office in about ten minutes.

Any pregnant woman is likely to face complex and conflicting thoughts and emotions as she ponders whether to have the baby, to carry the baby to term and then put it up for adoption, or to get an abortion. As the Boston Women's Health Book Collective explains, if a pregnancy is unplanned, women

> may be angry and sad that we don't have the money, relationship, or living situation that would allow us to go ahead and have a baby....

If we decide we most want to go ahead with the pregnancy, we will still have moments of resentment and fear and uncertainty. On the other hand, if we choose abortion there are also opposing feelings within us. ... If we already have children, there's the feeling that we know what a child of ours would be like, and it feels cruel to say no to that possibility. We may feel selfish.... We may feel guilty, especially if our religion disapproves of abortion or if we feel morally opposed to ending life.[1]

A study by the Alan Guttmacher Institute revealed that women are most likely to abort for these four reasons:

- They are unready for how a baby could change their life (most frequently they say that having a baby would interfere with work or school).
- They do not have enough money to bring up a baby.
- They either have problems with their relationship with their husband or partner, or they want to avoid being single parents.
- They are not ready for the responsibility.

Even if a pregnancy is planned, there are hard questions women may ask themselves. Should I be tested to determine whether my future child would be retarded or have a serious hereditary illness? Should I terminate the pregnancy if I get unhappy results on this test?

As long as abortion is available such dilemmas are dealt with according to the woman's personal ethics. She may consult her husband or partner, her pastor, her friends, or her mother, but the choice is hers.

The broader abortion debate, however, takes place not within a woman's conscience but in courts and legislatures, and is a matter of public ethics. The question here is whether society should let a pregnant woman have this choice or instead enact laws to protect the developing life within her. People who believe the fetus's right to live overrides the mother's autonomy say abortion should not be an option, or should be available only under very narrow circumstances. Those who feel that the mother's autonomy is paramount argue that the ethical questions surrounding abortion are for individual women to decide, free of government coercion.

In historical terms, attempts to outlaw abortion are relatively recent. The ancient Greeks and Romans permitted abortion in the early stages of pregnancy. During early Christianity abortion was allowed until forty days after conception (for a male fetus) or ninety days (for a female), the time when the fetus was believed to become "animated" by the "rational soul." In thirteenth-century England abortion was legal until "quickening," when the woman could first feel the fetus move, which took place at about twenty weeks.

Abortions were legal in the United States until the late 1800s. Then the states, anxious to protect women from the dangers of the procedure (it was not done safely then and many women died) and responding to the puritanical morality of the day, declared abortion a crime. It was not until the 1960s that they began to liberalize abortion laws.

The Supreme Court has played a key role in abortion law for almost two decades. The 1973 landmark case *Roe* v. *Wade* legalized abortions across the country. The Court ruled that a woman's constitutional right to privacy barred state governments from interfering if she wanted to terminate her pregnancy.

While a liberal majority of justices controlled the Court, subsequent decisions struck down most state attempts to limit abortion. The federal government and the states were permitted, however, to bar public funding for poor women's abortions. This made abortion much less accessible to impoverished women in most states. (Women faced similar economic barriers prior to *Roe*. In the two and a half years before that ruling, nearly 350,000 women traveled to New York, one of the few states where abortion was legal and available to nonresidents, to

"Jane Roe," subject of the landmark Supreme Court case *Roe v. Wade*, appeared at a prochoice rally in Washington, D.C., in 1989.

end their pregnancies. Such a trip would have been difficult if not impossible for those who could not afford bus fare.)

On July 3, 1989, the three conservative justices appointed by former President Ronald Reagan joined two others in a dramatic change of direction. While not overturning *Roe*, in *Webster v. Reproductive Health Services* the Court emphasized "the State's interest in protecting potential human life," and permitted states to limit abortion in ways not previously considered constitutional.[2]

The Supreme Court may eventually go even further and reverse its 1973 landmark decision. This would not, however, put the issue to rest; in a post-*Roe* world, neither the federal government nor the states would be required to restrict abortion. Voters would have an increasingly important role as they decided whether to elect representatives favoring or opposing legal abortion. As of this writing, the political winds that have long favored anti-abortion forces are changing direction. The U.S. Congress, as well as several states re-examining the issue in light of *Webster*, are showing a reluctance to limit access to abortion.

Public opinion is evenly divided on the issue. According to a July 1989 *New York Times*/CBS News Poll, 48 percent of Americans want abortion to remain legal as under the *Roe* decision; 39 percent think it should be legal only in cases of rape or incest or if the mother's life is in danger; and 9 percent believe it should not be legal under any circumstances.

Technology may also play an important role in shaping the abortion debate. A new drug called RU 486, which induces abortion early in a pregnancy, making surgery unnecessary, is now available in France and China. Its introduction in the United States would probably undermine opposition to abortion by making it a more private act.

On the other hand, inventions that could push back the age of fetal viability—the age at which the fetus can live outside the womb—would help the cause of those opposed to abortion. Under *Roe*, abortion is generally illegal in the last trimester (final three months) of pregnancy, because during that period the fetus becomes viable. One new technology, "liquid oxygen," might help very premature babies survive by bringing oxygen to their undeveloped lungs. If this experimental procedure works, it could make more fetuses viable in the second trimester, undermining the timetable set forth in *Roe*.

Though we can expect changes in the technological and legal context in which abortions take place, the different camps in the abortion debate base their positions on certain enduring principles. The following are some of their main arguments:

The Case for Abortion Rights: People favoring a woman's right to choose abortion—women's rights advocates, civil libertarians, and others—express a wide range of opinion on the subject. The most radical feminists in the "prochoice" movement see abortion as no different morally from other minor surgery, like having a mole removed. Others find the procedure morally acceptable but a loss nonetheless. And some are personally opposed to it and say it is wrong, but they believe that the individual woman should be allowed to decide this question for herself—without government interference.

Prochoice arguments rest largely on women's autonomy. Like men, women control their own bodies, freely deciding what to eat, whom to have sex with, what medical treatment to accept or refuse. Similarly, say advocates for choice, a woman's uterus is a private sphere and what happens there is her business, not the government's. According to this view, laws prohibiting abortion are as morally unacceptable as laws—such as those existing in China today—requiring it in certain cases.

Economics also comes into play. Poor women may become trapped in poverty by having children before they are finished with their education and able to get a well-paying job. A vicious cycle results when these children grow up and have babies early in their own lives. The availability of contraception and abortion, say its supporters, can help the poor out of this cycle. Singer Mary Travers calls the decision she made to have an illegal abortion as a poor, young, divorced mother not "a choice," but "a responsibility to both the child I already had and to myself."[3]

Some also consider legal abortion a matter of civil rights. As Supreme Court Justice Harry Blackmun wrote in his dissent in *Webster*: "Millions of women ... have ordered their lives around the right to reproductive choice, and ... this right has become vital to the full participation of women in the economic and political walks of American life."[4]

The Case Against Legal Abortion: People advocating laws that would restrict or eliminate legal abortion, often called "prolife," also approach the issue from a variety of perspectives. Many in the right-to-life movement have beliefs stemming from their religion—most often Catholic or Fundamentalist Protestant— while some act out of secular moral concerns. Whereas abortion opponents tend to be politically conservative, a minority on the left also believe the practice should be restricted.

Those who oppose abortion see the fetus—what they may call a "preborn child"—as human life, and therefore inherently precious and deserving of protection. "Abortion is contrary to all that life is," says the National Right to Life organization.[5] *Village Voice* columnist Nat Hentoff argues that women cannot defend killing a fetus in an abortion by pointing to their right to privacy. That would be like trying to justify the killing of a slave by saying he was not fully human and was "owned in privacy."[6]

The easy availability of abortion, say prolifers, has led many women to terminate their pregnancies casually rather than as a last resort to protect their health or save their life. They use abortion so they won't become single parents, because they aren't getting along well with their partner, or to avoid interrupting their careers or education. Some aren't conscientious about contraception and end up using abortion merely as a form of birth control.

Abortion opponents claim that these women are killing their fetuses for their own convenience, decreasing the dignity of, and respect for, all human life. This disregard, they say, leads to callousness toward other weak and dependent people, such as children, the sick, and the disabled.

FETAL RIGHTS VERSUS MATERNAL RIGHTS

In June 1987, Angela Carder, a twenty-eight-year-old married woman who had battled leukemia since age thirteen, was in her twenty-fifth week of pregnancy. When she started to experience shortness of breath and back pain, doctors at George Washington University Hospital ran tests and discovered a tumor in one of her lungs; they told her she had only a few days to live.

Carder requested that priority be given to making her feel comfortable in her last days. According to her mother, she said, "I only want to die, just give me something to get me out of this pain." Her husband, her mother, and most of her physicians believed that these desires should be respected.

But the hospital administration had a concern besides Carder's quality of life. They thought they might have a responsibility to save her fetus—which they believed could live outside of her body at this point—by performing a cesarean section. If she died first, the fetus's life would surely end with hers. Since she would not consent to the procedure, the hospital called in a judge to hear the case.

The lawyer appointed for the fetus argued that the state's interest in the fetus overrode the mother's rights because she had such a short time to live. But Carder's lawyer said she objected to surgery and that her wishes should be honored. The judge ruled, "It's not an easy decision to make, but given the choices, the court is of the view the fetus should be given an opportunity to live."

The cesarean was performed a few hours later. The baby lived for just two hours, and Carder died two days later.[7]

New technologies are creating opportunities for diagnosis and treatment of the fetus within its mother's womb. A technique called ultrasonography, for instance, gives doctors a "view" of the womb, letting them know if a vaginal delivery would endanger the fetus. If so, they may suggest that the patient undergo a cesarean section instead. Or they may demand it—as in Angela Carder's case.

At the same time, there is a new awareness of the effect of the pregnant mother's behavior on the development of her fetus. The many babies born addicted to crack cocaine are tragic testimony that if a mother abuses drugs, she may also be abusing her future child.

These developments have encouraged some people to think of the fetus as being distinct from its mother and having its own legal rights. One result of this is the "fetal rights" movement. The ethical conflicts and the debates over fetal rights are similar to those involving abortion. Fetal rights advocates demand that the fetus be given the same legal protection as the rest of us. In cases like Angela Carder's, the mother acts in a way that doctors say unnecessarily jeopardizes her fetus. Fetal rights advocates believe that when this happens, society should weigh the needs of the fetus against those of the mother to determine in whose interests to act.

Others, however, emphasize that the fetus is an inseparable part of a pregnant woman. To them a mother should be free to make decisions for both herself and her future child; and granting rights to the fetus as a separate being inevitably subordinates the woman's rights.

Most mothers will go to great lengths to ensure that their children will be healthy and sound, and most people would agree that if a mother plans to carry her pregnancy to term, she has an ethical obligation not to harm her fetus. But in some cases a woman will resist a doctor's demands, for instance, that she undergo a cesarean or not drink alcohol during pregnancy. Women's rights advocates insist that these mothers should be free to make their own decisions—wise or not—about their pregnancies. Fetal rights advocates, on the other hand, demand that in certain circumstances the state force women to take steps to protect the fetus.

Court-Ordered Cesarean Section

A recent survey published in *The New England Journal of Medicine* reported fifteen cases in eleven states in which doctors asked for court orders compelling a patient to undergo cesarean section. Judges agreed to issue the orders in thirteen of the cases. The authors concluded that such episodes are "an important and growing problem."[8]

Not all court-ordered cesareans involve tragic dramas like Angela Carder's, but many cases raise similar ethical problems. When a doctor orders a cesarean for the fetus's sake, a woman may object to the procedure because she's afraid of surgery or because she questions the need for it despite the doctor's advice. This is not necessarily irrational: a cesarean is a major surgical procedure and is somewhat riskier than a vaginal birth. And in several cases women fled to avoid forced surgery and gave birth naturally to healthy children; the doctors' diagnosis had been wrong. Some women also object to the surgery on religious grounds.

Another factor that makes some women wary of the procedure is that the percentage of babies delivered by cesarean section in the United States has greatly increased (about one in four deliveries is by cesarean). Many people believe the operation is often done needlessly by doctors who fear being sued if the baby is harmed during a vaginal delivery.

If it were just her life on the line, no one could compel any woman to undergo any treatment against her will. But since her choices affect the fetus, and some say the fetus has rights equal to hers, a conflict occurs.

Women's rights advocates are appalled by judges who order cesareans. Feminist writer Ellen Willis calls the forced surgery "medical rape"[9] and health law professor George J. Annas says it "degrades and dehumanizes the mother and treats her as an inert container."[10] In this view, if in some tragic cases a fetus dies unnecessarily, that's an acceptable price to pay for protecting women from having their bodies violated.

But advocates for fetal rights say that rather than degrading women, "these cases are testimony to a concern for the well-being of the fetus." They believe a pregnant mother should have legal responsibilities to her fetus that are comparable to her responsibilities to her existing children. Just as it is illegal to neglect children, goes this argument, it should be illegal to neglect a fetus. This will assure "that the unborn of today will be born tomorrow and ... that those born tomorrow will have the chance to live a whole or unimpaired life," writes law professor Jeffrey A. Parness.[11]

The courts have been split on the issue of forced cesareans. The leading decision came in the appeal of the Angela Carder case, after her death. The District of Columbia Court of Appeals ruled 7-1 that mothers should not be operated on against their will.[12] Writing for the majority, Judge John A. Terry argued that "To protect the right of every person to bodily integrity," everyone must be able to choose freely whether to accept or refuse medical treatment. He pointed out that the courts have refused to order people to donate organs or go through other intrusive surgery for the benefit of others. So how could the courts force a woman into major surgery to save a fetus, which hasn't even been born?

But in his dissenting opinion, Judge James A. Belson claimed that a woman carrying a viable fetus is in a unique position. "The expectant mother," he said, "has placed herself in a special class of persons who are bringing another person into existence, and upon whom that other person's life is totally dependent." Therefore, in deciding whether or not to require a woman to have a cesarean, the courts should strike a balance between the fetus's rights and the mother's rights.

Drugs and Fetal Rights

Several attempts have been made to criminally prosecute women who during their pregnancies take illicit drugs and do other things that might harm their fetuses. The cases raise issues similar to those in the cesarean debate. The most notorious one involved Pamela Rae Stewart of San Diego, who was arrested in 1986 for her alleged role in her baby's death. Stewart had a condition called "placenta previa," which places the fetus at risk for hemorrhage and oxygen deprivation. Against her doctor's advice, she used amphetamines and engaged in sexual intercourse while pregnant. Her baby was born with severe brain damage and lived for only six weeks.

Not all babies of drug-using mothers die. But those that survive may face addiction as infants and various other health problems later in life. According to estimates, each year 200,000 to 375,000 babies are born with drugs in their blood.

Criminal charges of child abuse against Stewart and other drug-using mothers have been dismissed as having no basis in law—the fetus is not legally considered a child. But people's outrage over the drug problem together with the strength of the anti-abortion movement may be changing this. A recent Gallup poll commissioned by *Hippocrates* magazine shows support for punishing pregnant mothers even when the drugs they take are legal. Forty-eight percent thought that tobacco- or alcohol-using pregnant women should be held legally liable for any harm done to their fetus; 42 percent disagreed.

California has considered legislation criminalizing such acts of "fetal neglect" when illegal drugs are involved, as well as mandatory drug testing of all pregnant women. Recently in Florida prosecutors won their first case against a mother by charging her with felony drug delivery to her child—for the 90 seconds when it was outside her body but still attached to the umbilical cord, receiving drug-laden blood. Several similar cases have been brought since then.

In February 1990, however, a judge in Laramie, Wyoming, dismissed a child abuse charge brought against a woman for drinking alcohol while pregnant. Pregnant women who drink excessively often give birth to children with a debilitating condition called "fetal alcohol syndrome." But the judge ruled there was no way of knowing if the drinking had harmed this particular fetus.

Women's rights advocates call for educating mothers about the dangers to their fetus of taking drugs during pregnancy, rather than punishing them. They worry that the fetal rights movement could significantly erode women's liberty by making "doctor's orders" law. Since so many things women do during pregnancy can affect a fetus, the legal enforcement of fetal rights would lead to behavior control and surveillance. Eve W. Paul, director of legal affairs for Planned Parenthood Federation of New York, points out that "in China government officials check up on women's menstrual periods."[13]

Even when drugs are involved, some feel it is unfair to prosecute pregnant addicts when what they really need is medical care—and very few treatment programs are geared to them. And health care workers say the threat of prosecution is counterproductive, frightening women away from such programs and even leading them to give birth at home. "They're afraid their babies will be taken away," says San Francisco deputy city attorney Lori Giorgi.[14]

But those who favor the law enforcement approach see it as the only way to stop pregnant women from using drugs and harming their babies. "The nice thing about jail is that moms get good prenatal care, good nutrition and they're clean [drug-free]," argues Dr. Jan Bays, director of Child Abuse Programs for Emanuel Hospital in Portland, Oregon.[15]

A law-enforcement official in Greenville, South Carolina, argues that there is nothing unfair about prosecuting a mother who uses drugs to the detriment of her fetus. She says it is different from prosecuting a nonpregnant person for being an addict. While she would not bring charges against an alcoholic for his or her addiction, "If an alcoholic gets in a car and drives drunk and kills somebody, who's going to tell me you don't prosecute that person criminally? To me it's the same thing."[16]

IN-VITRO FERTILIZATION

After Mary Sue Davis married Junior Lewis Davis in 1979, the Tennessee couple tried to have a child. But Mary Sue had five abnormal, "tubal" pregnancies instead.

In a tubal pregnancy the fertilized egg implants itself in a fallopian tube and does not reach the uterus. The condition is life-threatening. As a result of her tubal pregnancies, one of Mary Sue's fallopian tubes ruptured and the other had to be tied in surgery—preventing her from ever having a child by normal means.

Still determined, the couple went to the Fertility Center of East Tennessee in Knoxville, where they enrolled in an "in-vitro fertilization" program. In this procedure doctors use surgery to remove eggs from a woman's ovaries. These eggs are fertilized in a petri dish with her partner's sperm, creating embryos. After incubating for a few days, the embryos are inserted into the mother's uterus in the hope that one of them will become implanted there.

The efforts to implant two of the nine embryos conceived in vitro by the Davises failed. Later their marriage fell apart, and the couple filed for divorce. Meanwhile, the seven remaining embryos remained in storage, frozen in liquid nitrogen at the fertility center.

Now Mary Sue, twenty-nine, a former service representative for a Knoxville boat dealer, wants to use the embryos to become pregnant. But her thirty-year-old estranged husband, a refrigeration technician, no longer wants to be a father. He wants the embryos to remain frozen. The couple had not signed a contract specifying what would happen to the embryos if they got divorced.

At least 2.8 million couples in the United States would like to have children but cannot because of fertility problems. More and more of them, like the Davises, are turning to new technologies, such as in-vitro fertilization (IVF), so they can have the babies they so desperately want.

Since 1978, when the first infant conceived by in-vitro (literally, "in-glass") fertilization was born, more than 3,000 IVF babies have come into the world. Sometimes, as in the Davises' case, several embryos are frozen during the initial IVF procedure. They may be stored for a later pregnancy, donated to another infertile couple, or discarded. Maintained at a nippy −321° F (−196° C), they can last indefinitely in this state—600 years, according to one estimate. In 1985 there were 289 frozen embryos in the United States; by 1986 the number had grown to 824.

Although IVF has created a host of difficult ethical problems, few laws or government regulations restrict the procedure. One tough question, particularly when the freezing method is used, concerns the legal and moral status of the embryo. Is it a human being? Property? Or something else?

The Roman Catholic Church considers the embryo to be a human being from the moment it is conceived. A Catholic congregation has published a pamphlet on this issue that says, "The freezing of embryos, even when carried out in order to preserve the life of an embryo...constitutes an offense against the respect due to human beings by exposing them to grave risks of death or harm to their physical integrity, and depriving them, at least temporarily, of maternal shelter and gestation, thus placing them in a situation in which further offenses and manipulation are possible."[17]

But many disagree with this position. Bioethicist Peter Singer and Australian member of Parliament Deane Wells argue that an embryo has none of the minimal human capacities—consciousness, awareness of one's surroundings—that are the basis for someone having rights. Further, they claim there is no moral difference between an egg, a sperm, and the two when united in a three-day-old embryo. Each of these entities has the potential for life; eggs and sperm are not granted any rights; therefore the embryo shouldn't have any either.[18]

Some people believe that experimentation on human embryos up to fourteen days old is permissible. The reasoning is that at fourteen days embryos implant in the uterus and the development of the primitive nervous system begins. Before this point, many embryos are spontaneously flushed out of the mother's body. Thus a fourteen-day-old embryo has a far greater potential for becoming a person than any given sperm or egg. Another rationale is that until fourteen days the embryo may split, forming identical twins; it has no individual identity before then.

In the Tennessee case[19] Mary Sue Davis's attorney said at the divorce trial that her frozen embryos were "preborn children" who had rights of their own. But Junior Lewis Davis wanted the court to treat the case as a dispute over property, with each partner having equal rights to decide what became of the embryos. He contended that since he did not want to become a father for the time being, Mary Sue's use of the embryos would make him feel "raped of my reproductive rights."

At the trial John A. Robertson, a University of Texas law professor, testified that it is widely agreed that "the pre-embryo at this stage is not a legal subject. Because it represents potential life, it deserves a special respect above that accorded any other human tissue, but not the respect of a person."

But in what Judge W. Dale Young called "the toughest decision in my life as a judge," he decided to grant temporary custody of the embryos to Mary Sue. "The court finds that human life begins at the moment of conception," he ruled, calling the fertilized eggs not property but children—"human beings existing as embryos." He dealt with the case using the rules for traditional custody battles, in which the best interest of the child is given top priority.

Mary Sue reacted by saying, "I'm thrilled. It's definitely what I wanted." On the other hand, her husband complained, "They are going to force me to become a father against my wishes." He plans to appeal the decision.

The Davises employed in-vitro fertilization because Mary Sue, though fertile, was unable to conceive. Though the embryos were conceived artificially, the sperm and the eggs came from the couple planning to raise the child. This is the usual situation in which IVF is performed, but it is only one of several possibilities. If necessary, couples can also get donations of sperm, eggs, or embryos from other people so they can have a baby—and they can hire a "surrogate mother" to carry this baby in her womb for them.

These and other possible uses for IVF could dramatically change the way we view the family and raise many more legal, social, and ethical questions. For instance, if its genetic parents die, can a frozen embryo—born after being implanted in another woman—inherit their estate? Writer Martha A. Field worries that eventually people might be able to buy commercially available frozen embryos conceived from the egg and sperm of celebrities.

Just as startling, Field foresees a possible leap in the use of surrogate mothers. Surrogacy has been criticized for exploiting poor women, who, for a fee, carry in their womb a baby for another couple. IVF could make surrogacy more desirable by enabling both members of a couple to supply the genetic material for the baby without having to carry it. For instance, if Joe and Jane were each fertile and wanted to have a baby genetically tied to them, but Jane did not want to go through pregnancy and childbirth, they could use a surrogate. Jane's egg would be fertilized in a dish by Joe's sperm, and the resulting embryo could be transferred into the surrogate's uterus.

If there is an increase in the demand for surrogates, says Field, "The exploitation not only of the domestic poor but also of Third World women is likely to mushroom; it does not seem farfetched to imagine that there will one day be a thriving business of sending frozen sperm and frozen embryos around the world to be transferred to childbearers for the production of children for contracting couples."[20]

In this chapter we have looked at several issues surrounding pregnancy and birth. The status of the embryo or fetus on the one hand and the rights of the parents on the other have been consistent themes throughout. Fundamental questions were raised concerning the definition of human life, our moral obligations to it, and what role the law should play in this area.

The next two chapters similarly examine such basic questions—but at the opposite end of life's spectrum: death. As we will see, many of the controversies raised by care for the critically ill are strikingly parallel to those discussed in this chapter.

NOTES

1. Boston Women's Health Book Collective, *Our Bodies, Ourselves* (New York: Simon & Schuster, 1984), p. 222.

2. Linda Greenhouse, "High Court Upholds Sharp State Limits on Abortions," *The New York Times*, July 4, 1989, p. 10.
3. Mary Travers, "My Abortion, Then and Now," *The New York Times*, August 10, 1989, p. A23.
4. "A Woman's Right, Barely Viable" (editorial), *The New York Times*, July 4, 1989, p. 28.
5. John Lippis, "The Challenge to Be 'Pro Life'" (pamphlet; Washington, D.C.: National Right to Life Educational Trust Fund, 1982).
6. Nat Hentoff, "Dred Scott, Abortion, and Jesse Jackson," *The Village Voice*, February 21, 1989, p. 28.
7. George Annas, "She's Going to Die: The Case of Angela C," *Hastings Center Report*, February/March 1988, pp. 23–25.
8. Veronika E. B. Kolder, et al., "Court-Ordered Obstetrical Interventions," *The New England Journal of Medicine*, May 7, 1987, pp. 1192–1196.
9. Ellen Willis, "The Wrongs of Fetal Rights," *The Village Voice*, April 11, 1989, pp. 41–44.
10. George Annas, "She's Going to Die: The Case of Angela C," *Hastings Center Report*, February/March 1988, p. 24.
11. Jeffrey A. Parness, letter, *Hastings Center Report*, June 1987, p. 26.
12. Linda Greenhouse, "Court in Capital Bars Forced Surgery to Save Fetus," *The New York Times*, April 27, 1990, pp. A1, A18.
13. "Punishing Pregnant Addicts," *The New York Times*, September 10, 1989, p. E5.
14. Quoted in Susan LaCroix, "Jailing Mothers for Drug Abuse," *The Nation*, May 1, 1989, p. 586.
15. "Punishing Pregnant Addicts," *The New York Times*.
16. Jim Angle, report on fetal rights, *Morning Edition*, National Public Radio, August 24, 1989.
17. Congregation for the Doctrine of the Faith, "Respect for Human Life" (pamphlet; Boston: Daughters of St. Paul, not dated), p. 19.
18. Peter Singer and Deane Wells, *Making Babies* (New York: Scribners, 1985), pp. 73–74.
19. Quotes from Tennessee case are from "New Divorce Issue: Embryos' Status," *The New York Times*, August 8, 1989, p. A11; and Ronald Smothers, "Tennessee Judge Awards Custody of 7 Frozen Embryos to Woman," *The New York Times*, September 22, 1989, p. A13.
20. Martha Field, *Surrogate Motherhood* (Cambridge, Mass.: Harvard University Press, 1988).

ADDITIONAL SOURCES

Abortion

"Bitter Pill," *The Nation*, November 21, 1988, pp. 515–516.
Boston Women's Health Book Collective, *The New Our Bodies, Ourselves*, (New York: Simon & Schuster, 1984).
Richard D. Glasow, "New Study Confirms Women Abort for Social, Not Health Reasons," *National Right to Life News*, October 20, 1988, p. 12.
Rachel Benson Gold, *Abortion and Women's Health* (New York: The Alan Guttmacher Institute, 1990).
"Important Facts about Induced Abortion" (pamphlet; American College of Obstetricians and Gynecologists, 1985).
"Notes and Comment," *The New Yorker*, April 24, 1989, pp. 29–30.
Lynn M. Paltrow, "Threat to Women's Rights," *Civil Liberties* (newsletter; American Civil Liberties Union, Winter 1989), pp. 1, 7.

Fetal Rights versus Maternal Rights

George J. Annas, "Protecting the Liberty of Pregnant Patients," *The New England Journal of Medicine*, May 7, 1987, pp. 1213–1214.
"Child Abuse Charge Is Dismissed for Pregnant Woman Who Drank," *The New York Times*, February 3, 1990, p. 12.
Gregory L. Goyert, et al., "The Physician Factor in Cesarean Birth Rates," *The New England Journal of Medicine*, March 16, 1989, pp. 706–09.
Dawn Johnsen, "A New Threat to Pregnant Women's Autonomy," *Hastings Center Report*, August/September 1987, pp. 33–40.
Elaine Korry, report on fetal rights, *All Things Considered*, National Public Radio, May 13, 1989.
Ruth Macklin, *Mortal Choices* (Boston: Houghton Mifflin, 1987).
Walter K. Meeker, letter, *The New England Journal of Medicine*, November 5, 1987, p. 1224.
John A. Robertson and Joseph D. Schulman, "Pregnancy and Prenatal Harm to Offspring," *Hastings Center Report*, August/September 1987, pp. 23–32.
"Where Americans Draw the Line," *Hippocrates*, May/June 1988, pp. 40–41.

Most fetuses develop within their mother's womb for approximately nine months before being born. But occasionally, for a variety of reasons, a mother may give birth early in the pregnancy—sometimes so early that the baby isn't "viable": it hasn't developed enough to survive on its own. Many babies on the borderline live, thanks to technological advances in medicine. It wasn't always this way.

In early twentieth-century America, mothers gave birth at home, and even if their babies were premature and sick, that's where they cared for them. General practitioners, midwives, or obstetricians did their best to protect sick infants from infection. If their condition was poor, doctors couldn't do much besides wait for them to die.

This changed after World War II, when doctors set up special hospital units for premature babies. The units featured new treatment and care methods that were being successfully used with adults—such as feeding patients through tubes and providing antibiotics. Also, surgeons learned new procedures for operating on newborns.

The development of newborn intensive care in the early 1960s saved younger and younger infants from death. Eventually, technology allowed very premature infants—many born after being in the womb for less than twenty-eight weeks—to survive. In 1989 doctors began experimenting with putting an oxygen-carrying liquid into a premature baby's lungs; the procedure simulates conditions inside the womb. If it works, it could push back even further the age of fetal viability. The result of developments like these is described by Howard W. French:

> In a special section of the neonatal intensive-care ward, where the most dangerously premature children are kept, babies hardly larger than a hand are cared for by teams of nurses. Each is connected to a gaggle of monitoring devices. Gold heart-shaped thermometers; respirator tubes in tracheas; laser blood-oxygen sensors attached to feet; pulse-measuring gauges on chests; and the ubiquitous intravenous tubing that provides both nutrition and medication.[1]

CRITICALLY ILL BABIES

Though thousands of babies have been saved who would have doubtless died in the past, and many parents can be grateful, technology has proved to be a two-edged sword. The financial cost of saving these infants is often astronomical. They require expensive care early on—more than $100,000 worth in some cases; if they are permanently disabled, they may need special educational facilities as well as a lifetime of medical support. The parents may have to devote so much time to their care that they must work fewer hours or even give up their jobs. In addition, as an editorial in the *Journal of the American Medical Association* put it, "The costs in pain, grief, guilt, and other intangibles cannot be estimated."[2]

This is the backdrop to a special ethical dilemma created by the survival of so many sick babies: in cases where the outlook for the baby's health or life is poor, under what circumstances is it ethical to stop treatment and allow him or her to die? This problem first gained the American public's attention through the "Baby Doe" case.

Baby Doe (the name given to the infant in court to protect the family's privacy) was cared for in a hospital in Bloomington, Indiana, in April 1982. The infant had a birth defect—a blockage in the esophagus—that prevented Baby Doe from eating normally. Apparently because the baby also had Down syndrome, a form of mental retardation, the parents refused to allow doctors to do surgery to correct the esophagus problem. The hospital asked a court for permission to perform the surgery over the parents' wishes. The court refused, citing the parents' right to privacy and autonomy. The infant died at six days of age.

Some people agreed that decisions like this should be left to the parents. Others were furious that an infant who could have been saved was allowed to die. Among them were officials in the Reagan administration, who promptly issued regulations requiring treatment for disabled infants. One controversial rule required hospitals to post a telephone number in child-care wards that could be called if the regulations were disregarded. The new regulations were soon challenged, and a U.S. district

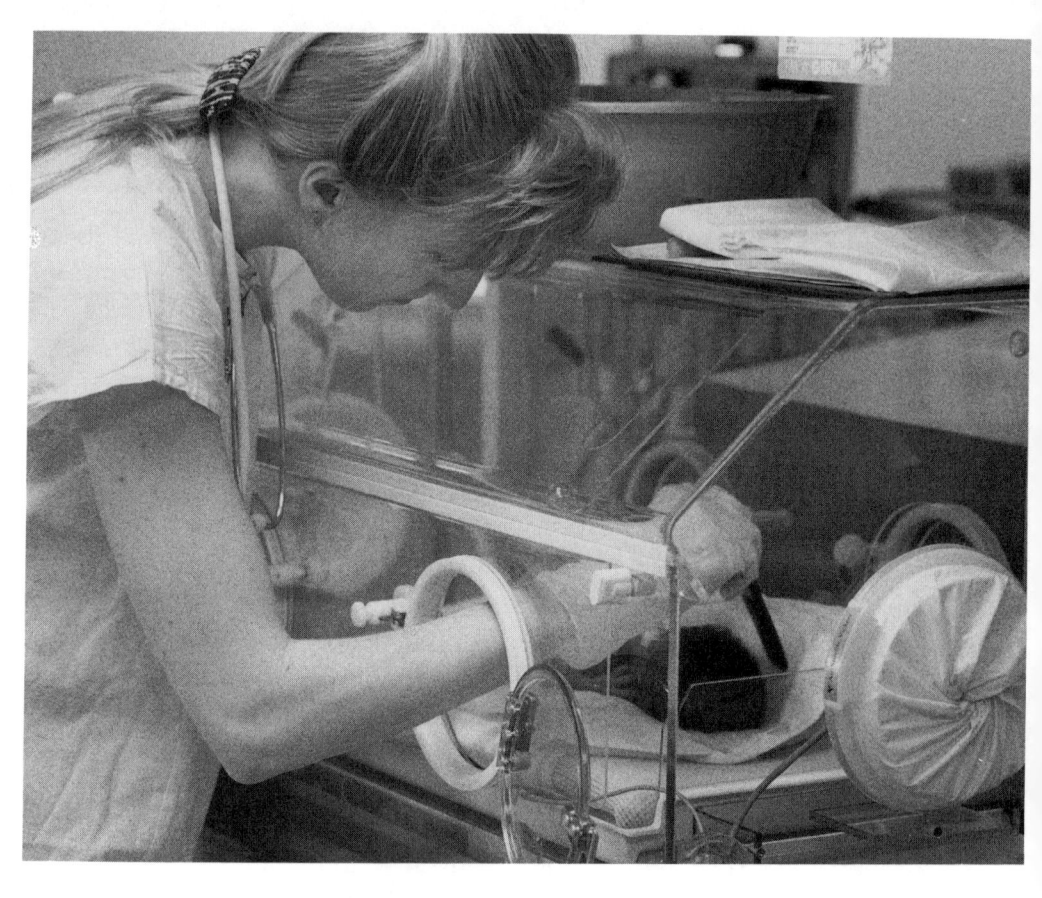

Care for premature and critically ill babies requires a great deal of dedication, time, and money.

judge struck them down. Modified regulations adopted by the administration require treatment of any disabled infant unless it is dying and beyond rescue or is in a coma, with no chance of regaining consciousness.

The ethical standard behind the Baby Doe regulations is known as the "sanctity of life"—one of several standards put forward in deciding on treatment for sick newborns. According to this standard, all infants, as human beings, have intrinsic worth and dignity; none of them should be denied treatment just because of a disability that could mean a low "quality of life" in the future. Had the Baby Doe rules been in effect at the time, doctors would have had to save the retarded infant from

Indiana—because they would have saved a nonretarded baby with the same stomach abnormality. Any other treatment would have discriminated against Baby Doe.

Some view the question as a matter of civil rights. *Village Voice* columnist Nat Hentoff argues that though many don't realize it, treating infants like Baby Doe differently is as morally unacceptable as discriminating against a baby because of its race: "If word got out that infanticide was being practiced solely on the basis that an infant was black, you'd hear about hardly anything else for weeks.... [But] there is something about the disabled ... that causes the press, and most other people, to avert their eyes."[3]

Similarly, members of some organizations advocating greater rights for disabled people feel that Baby Doe's struggle is their struggle. One such advocate from Boston, who is paralyzed, said, "We got into that fight because we knew that if society is not willing to assign a high value to a handicapped baby, then it will continue to have a low evaluation of the handicapped who *are* allowed into the world. If a Baby Doe doesn't have full rights, it's harder for us to get them."[4]

The sanctity-of-life position has traditionally been taken by members of orthodox religious groups that call themselves "pro-life" because they oppose abortion. But a small minority of Catholic theologians, as well as many secular bioethicists, are now using a different approach that involves factoring into the equation the infant's "quality of life." Those who emphasize the quality of life feel that in some cases keeping a baby alive is actually worse than allowing him to die. They might choose to terminate treatment and let the baby die, for instance, if he were in terrible pain, with no hope that it would be alleviated.

Another quality-of-life consideration that, to some ethicists, justifies termination of treatment arises when a baby is so grossly malformed that he cannot interact with others in any way. Jesuit priest Richard A. McCormick argues that "life is a value to be preserved only insofar as it contains some potentiality for human relationships." According to McCormick, when relationships are not possible, "it is neither inhuman nor unchristian" to withdraw treatment.[5] This view, like the sanctity-of-life view, would require treating Baby Doe—because even though the baby would have a permanent handicap, people with Down syndrome *can* have human relationships. But it would not require treating another baby with more severe disabilities who could not experience such relationships.

Complicating the quality-of-life perspective is the problem of medical uncertainty. In the story opening this chapter, a premature baby survived despite the doctor's expectations that he would not, illustrating that a diagnosis can be wrong in these cases. That story had a happy ending, but it could have had a tragic one, with the baby dying unnecessarily as a result of being taken off the respirator.

On the other hand, in some instances a diagnosis predicts that an infant's future will be bright when in reality the child will continue to be sick and in pain until his or her short life is over. Treatment is not withdrawn, and the infant's suffering is unnecessarily prolonged. As those who favor the quality-of-life standard see it, this kind of unnecessary suffering is the main drawback of the sanctity-of-life standard—which in all but the direst cases imposes a duty to treat the infant. The advantage of the sanctity approach, however, is that infants wrongly diagnosed as having a poor outlook will not die unnecessarily.

Another standard would allow Baby Doe to die despite the child's ability to have relationships with others. This standard looks at how much of a burden Baby Doe would be to the parents. According to the burden standard, if the financial and emotional costs would be too much for the family to handle, the family should be allowed to tell doctors to withdraw treatment.

"Only to the extent that society accepts the burden and responsibility of caring for the handicapped infant throughout its lifetime does it have the right to impose a decision on the parents of the handicapped infant," says Hugh A. Frank, M.D., of the University of San Diego School of Medicine.[6] Frank argues that the public institutions currently housing and caring for disabled children are not humane and that an infant might be better off dead than living in one of them.

The burden standard emphasizes the parents' needs. Thus it has a very different outlook from both the sanctity-of-life and quality-of-life standards, which are each concerned primarily with the child's needs, although in different ways.

NOTES

1. Howard French, "Tiny Miracles Become Huge Public Health Problem," *The New York Times,* February 19, 1989, p. 44.
2. Mildred Stahlman, "Implications of Research and High Technology for Neonatal Intensive Care," *Journal of the American Medical Association,* March 24/31, 1989, p. 1791.
3. Nat Hentoff, "Is It Discriminatory to Kill Handicapped Infants?" *The Village Voice,* March 11, 1986, p. 32.
4. Quoted in Nat Hentoff.
5. Quoted in Ruth Macklin, *Mortal Choices* (Boston: Houghton Mifflin, 1987), p. 124.
6. Hugh A. Frank, "Whose Interests, Whose Burdens?" (letter), *Hastings Center Report,* October/November 1988, p. 51.

ADDITIONAL SOURCES

John D. Arras et al., "The Effect of New Pediatric Capabilities and the Problem of Uncertainty," *Hastings Center Report,* December 1987, pp. 10–13.

John D. Arras et al., "Standards of Judgment for Treatment," *Hastings Center Report,* December 1987, pp. 13–16.

Cynthia B. Cohen et al., "A History of Neonatal Intensive Care and Decisionmaking," *Hastings Center Report,* December 1987, pp. 7–9.

Gina Kolata, "For Babies, 'Liquid Air' May Spare Fragile Lungs," *The New York Times,* August 29, 1989, p. C3.

CHAPTER SIX

CRITICALLY ILL ADULTS AND THE "RIGHT TO DIE"

NOBODY wants to think about dying. Confronting one's own mortality is difficult and painful. Yet modern technology, because of its ability to artificially prolong human life beyond its natural span, has made it more important than ever to individuals and societies to come to terms with death. Is living with unbearable suffering or in a vegetative state worse than dying? Should an individual be allowed to decide that his or her life is no longer worth living and have doctors disconnect life-sustaining equipment? Should doctors play an active role in helping patients to die? These are some of the tough questions forced on us by advances in medical care.

Those who usually answer no to these questions emphasize the sanctity of human life. They worry that a society that lets people die, or kills them, in the medical arena will lose its respect for human life in general. They see current trends in allowing patients to die as leading to a world where the fittest survive, the weak perish, and people with disabilities are not tolerated.

People who feel that the terminally ill and the permanently unconscious should be allowed to die emphasize individual autonomy and the quality of life. They worry that if we, as individuals, are not given the freedom to make our own life-or-death decisions, we will become slaves, not masters, of medical technology. The result will be a grisly scene: hospitals filled with human vegetables, surviving indefinitely and draining our resources.

We can all agree that the nightmare visions of both camps are extremely disturbing. It is crucial that we understand their arguments so we can take steps to prevent either vision from turning into a reality.

WITHDRAWING TREATMENT

In the last two decades there has been a strong trend in medicine toward giving patients more and more control over their own care. Now they can refuse care, and doctors will respect their wishes even if it means death. In one case a court went as far as upholding a woman's right to refuse food; she was being fed through a tube. This is the closest a court had ever come to permitting euthanasia, which is discussed later in this chapter.

The societal consensus about the right to end care is shown in a Gallup poll commissioned by *Hippocrates* magazine in 1988. People were asked, "Under what circumstances would you say that a terminally ill person has the right to have treatment stopped so that he or she may die?" Ninety percent felt that treatment could be stopped if the doctor thought it best; 83 percent agreed if the patient was in great pain; 81 percent agreed if the patient's family went along with the decision; and 63 percent agreed under any circumstances. Only 7 percent felt that "The patient has *no* right to stop treatment under any circumstances."[1]

But what about patients who are unconscious or otherwise "incompetent" to make decisions and cannot make their wishes known? Should every effort be made to keep them alive? Should families be allowed to terminate their care? This is an extremely complex problem.

Over the last hundred years doctors' options in treating critically ill patients have greatly increased. Before then they had only crude painkillers and other basic medical tools available, and were limited to keeping watch over and comforting their dying patients. Now, thanks to technology, they have the ability to greatly prolong life. But this has been a mixed blessing.

Machines such as respirators can now keep alive indefinitely people with terminal illnesses or severe brain damage—who not that long ago would have gone to their graves much earlier. But the quality of their technology-dependent lives may be miserable. This has raised a host of ethical problems all related to the question: At what point can doctors "pull the plug" and let patients die?

The landmark court case that brought this issue to the public's attention was decided in 1975 in New Jersey. Karen Ann Quinlan, 21, had lapsed into a "persistent vegetative state" (PVS) after consuming a combination of tranquilizers and alcohol. Someone in this condition is permanently unconscious and is totally unaware of herself or her environment. She may survive indefinitely; the longest reported survival of a person in PVS was 37 years, 111 days. Today there are about 10,000 PVS patients in the United States.

Because Karen had no chance of recovery, her parents wanted to take her off the respirator that artificially helped her breathe. Their daughter, they said, would not want to live like this. A New Jersey court agreed, ruling that the right to refuse treatment increased as the "degree of bodily invasion increases and the prognosis dims."[2] Because a respirator is invasive (it forces air into and out of the lungs) and Karen's unconsciousness was permanent, the court ordered doctors to withdraw the respirator. At this point she started breathing on her own and

Karen Ann Quinlan's parents, after a long battle in court, won the right to have Karen Ann's respirator withdrawn.

survived in her unconscious state for another ten years, sustained by intravenous feeding.

Treatment for critically ill adults raises ethical questions similar to those brought up by the Baby Doe issue discussed in Chapter 5. As in the treatment of babies, there is a debate over standards of care. Some people take the sanctity-of-life position that preserving human life is always good. This is opposed to the quality-of-life standard, which determines whether a person's life should be preserved based on her ability to interact with the environment, to give or receive love, to make choices—namely, to be truly human. Quinlan's parents felt that the quality of their daughter's life did not justify continued treatment.

Patient autonomy comes into the picture, however, when the person is an adult. Unlike infants, who have no "wishes," an adult can make her wishes known in advance of an illness. She can do this in several ways. First, while she is alert and aware, she can sign a document called a "living will" that expresses her wishes for treatment in the event she becomes "incompetent"—cannot make decisions—in the future. Or she can appoint a loved one to be a "proxy," to make decisions for her should she become incompetent.

Sometimes even if the patient has not designated a specific proxy, the courts will allow a family member to make decisions for an unconscious person—as was done in the Quinlan case. Such a family member is supposed to support the patient's autonomy by using "substituted judgment"—making decisions for the incompetent patient based on what that patient would have wanted, *not* on what the proxy would want. The theory behind this practice is that family members have spent their lives with the patient and know his or her wishes better than any doctor or court could.

Only 9 percent of Americans have signed a living will. This may be partly because doctors are reluctant to discuss the subject with their patients. Forty states and the District of Columbia have laws recognizing such wills as legal. Seventeen states allow for the designation of medical proxies.

Since the Quinlan case, state courts have generally weighed the state's interest in preserving life against the individual's right to refuse medical care he or she doesn't want. The courts and the rest of society have formed a consensus that it is not morally necessary to take "extraordinary" or "heroic" measures to save the life of a terminally ill or permanently unconscious patient. Doctors may refrain from resuscitating such a patient if she has a heart attack, from providing dialysis if her kidneys fail, or from providing artificial respiration—as in the Quinlan case. But defining what constitutes extraordinary or heroic care isn't always so easy.

Although Joseph Quinlan, Karen's father, fought to withdraw the respirator, when he was asked if he wanted her intravenous feeding stopped, he said, "Oh no, that is her nourishment."[3] When, if ever, feeding can be stopped is one of the thorniest questions raised in care for the critically ill. There is no consensus on the answer. In addition to intravenous feeding, a patient who cannot eat on her own may be fed artificially through a tube surgically implanted in the stomach, or a tube inserted through the nose and reaching down into the digestive tract.

Some people don't distinguish morally between artificial nutrition and, say, the artificial breathing induced by a respirator: just as humans don't naturally breathe using a machine, they don't naturally eat through a tube. Technology is keeping them alive either way. It is therefore just as permissible to withdraw a feeding tube as a respirator in order to let the patient die. What kills the patient is the underlying condition that has made her sick; she is not starved to death.

Others feel a distinction is crucial: yes, using respirators might be considered an "extraordinary" measure because people don't ordinarily rely on them—they breathe spontaneously. But feeding is different. It is basic human care, not medical care. "The feeding of the hungry is the most fundamental of human relationships,"[4] says bioethicist Daniel Callahan.

At certain times in our lives, such as childhood, we all rely on others to give us food. If a parent fails to provide food for her child, she is guilty of a crime—neglect. The removal of a feeding tube does not "allow" a person to die, some say, but actually kills her. For these people, it is no more morally acceptable than intentionally giving a patient an overdose of morphine to end her life. When a respirator is removed, a patient may die from an illness taking its inevitable course. But when feeding is halted, she starves.

Many ethicists, though uncomfortable about the withdrawal of artificial nutrition from an incompetent patient, feel it is warranted in some circumstances—for instance, when a patient who has lost consciousness has made it clear ahead of time that she would not have wanted to be fed through tubes. The American Medical Association and the American Association of Neurological Surgeons both have guidelines that allow for the termination of artificial nutrition in certain instances.

Most courts have let doctors withdraw feeding from an unconscious patient under these conditions:

- The patient had previously indicated that this was her preference.
- The patient had appointed a proxy, who requested the withdrawal.
- The family believes this is what the patient would have wanted.

Some courts, however, like the Supreme Court of Missouri, have not permitted the withdrawal of nutrition.

THE CASE OF NANCY CRUZAN

In 1983 Nancy Cruzan, then 25, of Missouri, was in a car accident.[5] A paramedic found her by the side of the road and performed resuscitation. Though her life was saved, Nancy, described as being "vivacious, outgoing, independent" before the incident, suffered severe brain damage and eventually was diagnosed as being in a persistent vegetative state. Doctors said she could survive indefinitely in this state—as long as thirty years. Since then she has been kept alive by a feeding tube surgically implanted in her stomach.

Cruzan's parents have been engaged in a long legal battle to remove the feeding tube so that their daughter, now 31, can die. Joe Cruzan, Nancy's father, said, "We have a situation here, a hopeless existence. There's no point in continuing treatment, and I think that artificial nutrition and hydration should be stopped." The parents argued that under the constitutional right to privacy, family members should be allowed to make this kind of decision without outside interference. As Missouri bioethicist Father Kevin O'Rourke put it, "The assumption that one needs state permission to make decisions for an incompetent loved one is preposterous."

But Donald Lamkins, director of the Missouri Rehabilitation Center, where Nancy is a patient, said, "We know we can unplug a machine [such as a respirator]. That isn't nearly so hard for us to accept. But the fact that we starve somebody to death? We don't do that." And James S. Cole, former president of the Missouri Citizens for Life, the state affiliate of the National Right to Life Committee, declared, "Our view is that the state must protect human beings from conception until natural death. Miss Cruzan is nowhere near a natural death. She has a handicap, and people shouldn't be starved to death because of a handicap."

In a 4–3 decision, the Missouri Supreme Court ruled against ending artificial feeding. Judge Edward Robertson, Jr., began his ruling, "Only the coldest heart could fail to feel the anguish of these parents who have suffered terribly these many years. They have exhausted any wellspring of hope which might have earlier accompanied their now interminable bedside vigil."

But the court noted that the state had adopted a pro-life policy when it passed an anti-abortion law stating that life begins at conception. This policy overcame any individual rights unless treatment was "oppressively burdensome." The feeding tube had been inserted when doctors thought Nancy might have a chance to recover; the court said that the continuation of feeding through this tube is not a burden. And it is not a "heroic" rescue effort: "Common sense tells us that food and water do not treat an illness, they maintain a life."

Taking a sanctity-of-life position, the court said that the state has an "unqualified interest" in the life of unconscious patients, regardless of its quality. "Were quality of life at issue, persons with all manner of handicaps might find the state seeking to terminate their lives."

Although Nancy Cruzan had never signed a living will, according to testimony she had had a "somewhat serious conversation" when she was 25 with a friend in which she said "she would not wish to continue her life unless she could live at least halfway normally." The court found the testimony "inherently unreliable."

The Cruzan family appealed to the U.S. Supreme Court, which upheld the Missouri court's decision.[6] Writing for the majority, Chief Justice William Rehnquist said the case presented "a perplexing question with unusually strong moral and ethical overtones." The Court found that a constitutional right to die does exist, and is protected by the Fourteenth Amendment, which guarantees "liberty." The amendment gives people the right to refuse medical treatment even if death results, according to the ruling.

However, the five-to-four majority agreed with the Missouri court that there was no "clear and convincing evidence" that Nancy Cruzan would have wanted treatment terminated under the circumstances. If she had signed a living will saying as much, Missouri would have been required to comply with her wishes. But since the individual states have an interest in "the protection and preservation of human life," they are free, absent such explicit instructions, to refuse a request by relatives to let a permanently unconscious person die. The ruling encouraged the use of living wills.

The Supreme Court has essentially left it up to the states to determine, through legislation or court cases, when treatment can be terminated in situations where a PVS patient had not made her wishes clear before losing consciousness. Only New York and Maine are as strict as Missouri about the evidence they require to establish a patient's intent. Therefore, the Cruzan family is considering having Nancy moved to a different state, where her feeding tube could be removed.

Complicating the argument in cases like these are misunderstandings about the PVS diagnosis itself. Some health care workers who tend to PVS patients claim that these people sometimes respond to their ministrations. A registered nurse caring for Nancy Cruzan claimed there were reports that Nancy had cried after someone read a Valentine card to her.

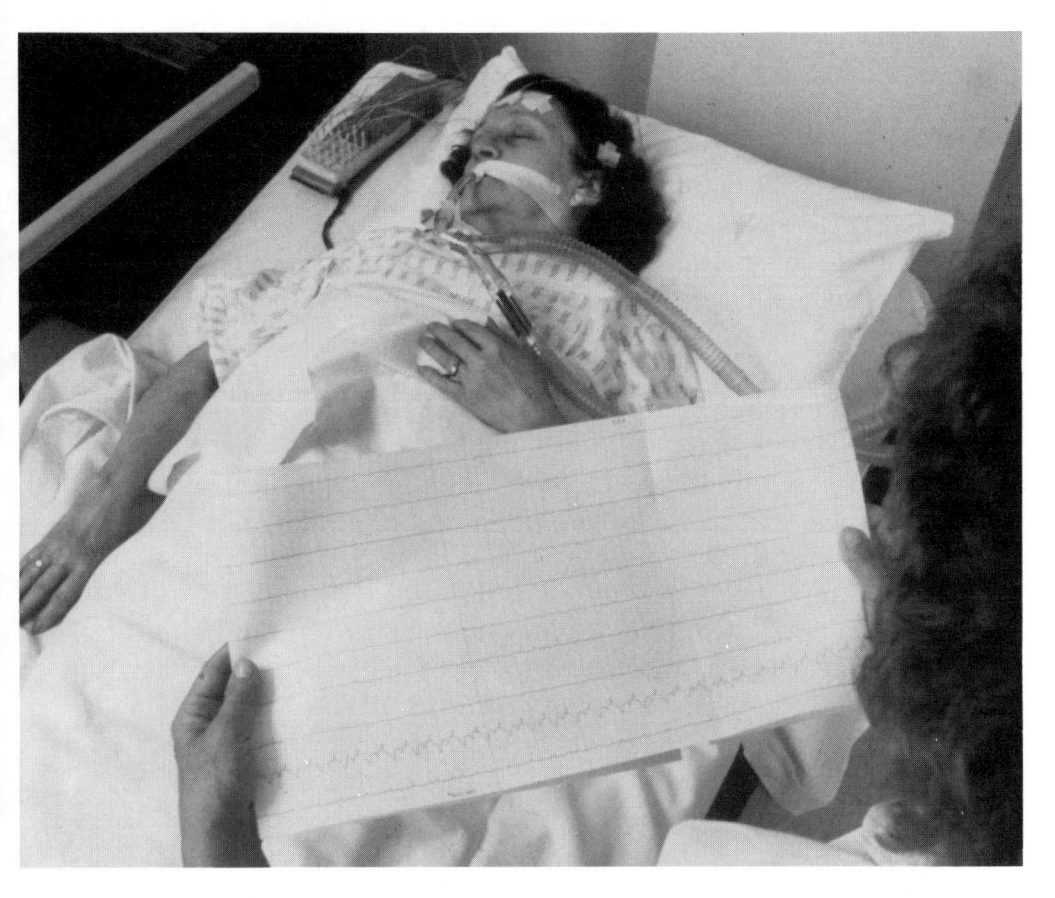

A patient whose electroencephalogram (EEG) test shows no brain activity is considered "brain dead."

But if a person is really in a persistent vegetative state, such seeming "reactions" are mere coincidences, initiated by a primitive part of the brain and having nothing to do with emotion. As Paul Armstrong, the lawyer who represented the family of Karen Quinlan, and B. D. Colen, the science editor of New York *Newsday*, put it, PVS patients "are not, as those in the 'Right to Life' movement would have us believe, 'handicapped' or 'disabled.' . . . They are unable to give or . . . perceive love on even the most primitive of levels. Rather, they are [nonthinking] organ systems, artificially sustained like valued [cells] in cancer laboratories."[7]

On the other hand, what if a diagnosis of PVS is a mistake?

What if that crying isn't the product of a nurse's imagination, if the tears are heartfelt? In a hospital in Albany, New York, 86-year-old Carrie Coons, diagnosed as being in a persistent vegetative state, was receiving food through a tube.[8] Her 88-year-old sister wanted to discontinue artificial feeding. She testified that Carrie—"a strong-willed religious woman . . . an energetic, vibrant person who enjoyed outdoor activities, including boating, camping, fishing and gardening"—would not want to be kept alive artificially.

The day after the judge ruled that the feeding should stop, Carrie woke up and spoke. The PVS diagnosis had been wrong. When questioned about her wishes, she expressed uncertainty about whether her feeding should stop if she became unconscious again.

Of course, any medical diagnosis can be wrong. But in many different situations doctors must make life-or-death decisions based on diagnoses that are less than 100 percent certain. Bioethicist Bruce Jennings argues that when done properly, the PVS diagnosis is as accurate as any in medicine. He says the lesson of the Coons case is that this diagnosis should be done carefully and the decision to terminate artificial nutrition and hydration should not be made too quickly. As for Cruzan, Jennings says, "She's had the best diagnostic techniques applied to her. It's been such a long period of time. There simply is no reasonable doubt left" that she is in a persistent vegetative state.[9]

EUTHANASIA

Jean Humphry was terminally ill with advanced cancer. Her husband, Derek Humphry, helped her commit suicide, and wrote this account of the event:

"I said that the doctor friend in London had given me something which was quite lethal . . . .

"We spent an emotionally charged morning together talking and holding each other. At one point Jean applied her makeup and

CRITICALLY ILL ADULTS AND THE "RIGHT TO DIE" 75

lipstick, tidied up her sidetables, and gave me instructions about what to do with her clothing and personal effects. . . .

"Jean [wanted] me to see her father after her death. 'Tell him exactly how I died' she said. 'I don't want him to think I died in pain or like a vegetable. He suffered enough when Mother died because no one would make any decisions. I want him to be sure to know I died this way.'

" . . . I left the room, mixed the drugs into a cup of coffee and returned to her bedside.

"'Is that it?' she asked. I nodded.

"I took her in my arms and kissed her.

"'Goodbye, my love.'

"'Goodbye, darling.'

"Jean lifted the mug and gulped down the contents completely. . . . Jean breathed heavily . . . and then died as I sat watching."*

Euthanasia means "good death." Here we will use the word in its more specific modern sense: the act, done out of mercy by a doctor, of ending someone's life. *Nonvoluntary euthanasia* is performed on incompetent patients, such as those suffering from advanced senility or in a permanent vegetative state. In this act a doctor actively causes the patient's death—for instance, by giving the patient a lethal injection. Some people see no moral difference between giving a patient a drug that will kill him and withdrawing the feeding tube.

Voluntary euthanasia is requested by a suffering, terminally ill patient who would rather die than continue to live in that condition. In this act a doctor directly gives the patient deadly drugs. In *assisted suicide* a doctor prescribes drugs like sleeping pills, in the knowledge that the patient plans to overdose on them.

Suicide is not illegal in this country, but euthanasia is illegal and assisting suicide is usually a crime. The law makes no exceptions for cases in which the deed was requested by the

*Derek Humphry, *Let Me Die Before I Wake* (Los Angeles: The Hemlock Society, 3rd ed., 1984), pp. 16–17.

person killed, the victim was suffering greatly, or the condition was hopeless. In several famous cases people have violated such legal prohibitions.

For instance, in June 1973 a man was left permanently paralyzed below the neck by a motorcycle accident and pleaded with his brother to end his life.[10] The brother returned to the hospital three days later with a sawed-off shotgun and said, "Close your eyes now, I'm going to shoot you." Then he pointed the weapon at the accident victim's head and pulled the trigger. The jury found the killer not guilty by reason of temporary insanity.

Juries in general have been reluctant to hand down murder convictions for people who end the lives of a suffering relative. Even those who champion the cause of euthanasia, however, do not condone this kind of "mercy killing" because it is done by non-medical personnel in cases where the patient is not terminally ill.

Some doctors also violate the laws against euthanasia and assisted suicide, although no one knows how many. It is likely that most of them never get caught; those who do are usually acquitted. One doctor has openly challenged such laws, creating a storm of controversy. In June 1990 retired pathologist Jack Kevorkian, upon the request of a woman with Alzheimer's disease, connected her to a homemade suicide device. She then pushed a button and the machine released a lethal dose of poison into her veins.

In 1988 the group Americans Against Human Suffering (AAHS) sponsored a referendum in California to legalize voluntary euthanasia by protecting from prosecution doctors who help their patients die. Called the Humane and Dignified Death Act, the proposal said,

> Self-determination is the most basic of freedoms. The right to die at the time and place of our own choosing when we are terminally ill is an integral part of our right to control our own destinies. . . . Modern medical technology has made possible the artificial prolongation of human life beyond natural limits. This prolonga-

tion of life for persons with terminal conditions may cause loss of patient dignity and unnecessary pain and suffering, while providing nothing medically necessary or beneficial to the patient.[11]

Under the measure, a patient who was diagnosed by two doctors as having less than six months to live could ask for a lethal injection. A physician morally opposed would not have to grant the request himself, but the patient would be free to seek one who would comply with his wishes. Any physician who did so would be protected from prosecution.

At the time, polls showed that 62 percent of Californians favored making voluntary euthanasia legally available. AAHS also did a survey of 600 California physicians who had treated patients with terminal illnesses. According to the organization, a majority said they "considered voluntary euthanasia to be a rational choice for their patients."[12] Although the California Medical Association opposed the initiative, in 1987 the California Bar Association had approved a measure supporting euthanasia.

However, the referendum's sponsors failed to get the number of petition signatures needed to get it on the ballot. They attributed the failure to poor organization and vowed to introduce the measure again—not only in California, but also in Washington, Oregon, and Florida.

Advocates of euthanasia have achieved success in the Netherlands, where a 1984 Dutch Supreme Court decision allowed the practice in certain approved circumstances. Between 5,000 and 10,000 lethal injections are now given there each year. To protect patients, euthanasia is permitted only if they are hopelessly ill, in unrelievable pain or discomfort, are rational and fully informed, and ask for death several times. Two doctors must agree to go along with the patient's wishes.

In this country it is likely that the debate over euthanasia will heat up as efforts to legalize it intensify. This is one issue in medical ethics that many Americans not trained in either medicine or ethics may eventually vote on directly. Because euthanasia is an emotional subject, it may be hard to make a rational judgment about whether the practice should be sanctioned. This makes it crucial to know and understand the logic of the arguments put forth by the opposing camps.

We have already compared the withdrawal of artificial feeding, which is highly controversial, with the termination of other forms of life support such as respirators, which is less so. In what ways, if any, is euthanasia morally different from "letting the patient die" by not resuscitating her or by withdrawing life-preserving equipment?

Some argue that there is no difference. They say that since suffering, terminally ill patients are allowed to exercise their autonomous choice by seeking death through a withdrawal of treatment, they should similarly be allowed to ask for a doctor's direct aid in dying. Ethicist James Rachels believes sometimes the latter course can be morally preferable. Take, for instance, the case of a patient with incurable throat cancer who has only a few days to live. The pain he is going through is unbearable, and the doctors cannot control it. When he asks his physician to withdraw treatment so he can die sooner, the doctor agrees, believing there's no reason to prolong the patient's suffering.

But if the doctor had, upon request, given him a lethal injection instead of merely withdrawing treatment, he would have been put out of his misery even sooner. Since the goal was to end the agony as soon as possible, wouldn't it have been preferable for the doctor to actively end the patient's life? As Rachels puts it, "Being 'allowed to die' can be relatively slow and painful, whereas being given a lethal injection is relatively quick and painless."[13]

It is true that high doses of painkillers can control almost anyone's pain until death. But these drugs may induce a stupor or unconsciousness. To euthanasia advocates, remaining in such a state until you die robs you of your dignity. They feel the choice between suffering terrible pain or being dazed and out of it is unacceptable. The terminally ill must have another option—dying with dignity, when they choose, with the aid of a physician.

In spite of these arguments, opposition to euthanasia in some quarters remains strong. The American Medical Association disapproves of it, and it is illegal in most countries. This opposition has historic roots: The Hippocratic oath, an ethical code formulated in ancient Greece that some medical school graduates still swear to, says, "I will neither give a deadly drug to anybody if asked for it, nor will I make a suggestion to this effect."[14]

Euthanasia opponents believe a doctor's responsibility is to make the dying patient more comfortable. To do this, many believe it is permissible to administer doses of painkiller that will, over a period, have the effect of decreasing a patient's life span. This is because the intent is to reduce pain, not to kill. The shortened life span is an unintended side effect. Others worry that giving high doses of narcotics to ease pain is too close, morally, to euthanasia, if the doctor believes it will hasten death.

All euthanasia opponents agree, however, that when a lethal dose is given intentionally to kill the patient, an ethical line is crossed. "The injunction not to kill is part of a total effort to prevent the destruction of human beings and of the human community," says ethicist Arthur Dyck. "It is an absolute prohibition in the sense that no society can be indifferent about the taking of human life."[15]

Some writers have drawn a distinction between a single *act* of euthanasia and a *policy* permitting the widespread practice of euthanasia. An act of euthanasia may be morally permissible in certain circumstances. In spite of this, as a matter of policy we must prohibit such an act. Our policy should express our principles against killing and prevent the bad consequences that would result from the acceptance of euthanasia.

One consequence euthanasia opponents fear is a general decrease in respect for human life. They make what is known as the "slippery slope" argument. Once society starts down the slippery slope by allowing an exception to the ancient commandment "Thou shalt not kill," it becomes harder and harder to stop the slide—it is irresistibly tempting to permit further exceptions.

Therefore, what started out as an effort to give people more control over their life and death could lead to the killing, for instance, of newborns with birth defects, people with Alzheimer's disease, or those who don't have medical insurance, simply because their treatment is emotionally or financially burdensome. As one observer put it, "Some are proposing what is called euthanasia; at present only a proposal for killing those who are a nuisance to themselves; but soon to be applied to those who are a nuisance to other people."[16]

Euthanasia opponents like legal scholar Yale Kamisar often recall Nazi Germany when making the slippery slope argument.[17] The Nazis, they say, began their genocidal drive for racial purity with a propaganda campaign to allow euthanasia of the severely ill. Eventually people who were unproductive, dissidents, the racially "impure," and finally anyone who wasn't German were added to the list of those unworthy to live.

Euthanasia advocates say it would be ridiculous to prohibit an act just because abuse of it is a possibility. As ethicist Daniel Maguire argues, this kind of logic would require the banning of scientific experiments involving humans. There have been many stories of unethical scientists putting volunteers in grave danger or actually harming them. But there is no clamor to end experimentation on humans, Maguire says, since experimental medicine serves a good purpose when done properly. Rather, as with euthanasia, abusers should be punished and abuses safeguarded against.

There are other, practical objections to euthanasia. Concern over the doctor-patient relationship is one of them. "How could a vulnerable, disabled patient be sure that the doctor approaching the bedside with a syringe was there to help and not to kill?" asks ethicist Mark Siegler.[18] Then the problem arises of whether the patient really means it when she asks for euthanasia—what if it is just a temporary depression that is making her ask to die?

Finally, doctors do make mistakes and no diagnosis of terminal illness is certain; if the practice were legal, someone could be "euthanized" who wasn't really terminally ill after all.

To answer the first two objections, euthanasia proposals often include a variety of safeguards, such as the requirement that two doctors approve of the procedure and there be a thirty-day waiting period after the patient's request. As for the possibility of misdiagnosis: as with any other medical procedure, the patient must make a decision based on the risks and benefits involved. The patient may decide that the relief of pain by death is a benefit that outweighs the minor risk that the diagnosis is incorrect.

In the two areas of reproduction and death, many parallel ethical issues are raised. It is not surprising that people who are opposed to abortion and in favor of fetal rights tend also to be against euthanasia and against withdrawing treatment from the critically ill. Those favoring abortion and maternal rights, on the other hand, usually also advocate the right to die. Generally, the controversies in both of these areas pit the principle of autonomy against the sanctity of human life.

Those who call themselves prolife see an embryo or a person who is permanently unconscious as "one of us"—an important member of the human community whose life it would be immoral to deny. They also may believe patients have a *responsibility* to the human community to stay alive as long as possible. People advocating "choice" in these matters have a different perspective. They look at the woman who doesn't welcome her pregnancy, the terminally ill person in great pain who wants to die, and say, it is not the prerogative of the human community to tell these people how to live or die.

NOTES

1. "Where Americans Draw the Line," *Hippocrates*, May/June 1988, p. 41.
2. Linda Greenhouse, "Does Right to Privacy Include Right to Die?," *The New York Times*, July 25, 1989, p. A15.

3. Daniel Callahan, "On Feeding the Dying," *Hastings Center Report*, October 1983, p. 22, reprinted in Robert F. Weir, ed., *Ethical Issues in Death and Dying* (New York: Columbia University Press, 1986), pp. 230–233.
4. Daniel Callahan, "On Feeding the Dying," p. 231.
5. Information and quotes on the Cruzan case are from Linda Greenhouse, "Does Right to Privacy Include Right to Die?"; "Missouri High Court in Shocking Reversal," *Society for the Right to Die Newsletter*, Spring 1989, p. 4; Nat Hentoff, "The Judge Who Would Not Kill," *The Village Voice*, June 13, 1989, p. 20; Nat Hentoff, "Would You Kill Nancy Cruzan?" *The Village Voice*, June 6, 1989, p. 19.
6. Linda Greenhouse, "Justices Find a Right to Die," *The New York Times*, June 26, 1990, pp. A1, A19.
7. Paul W. Armstrong and B. D. Colen, "From Quinlan to Jobes: The Courts and the PVS Patient," *Hastings Center Report*, February/March 1988, p. 39.
8. Nat Hentoff, "The Woman Who Escaped Her Right to Die," *The Village Voice*, June 20, 1989, p. 22.
9. Interview with Bruce Jennings, associate for policy studies at the Hastings Center, February 13, 1990.
10. Tom L. Beauchamp and James F. Childress, "Killing and Letting Die," excerpt from *Principles of Biomedical Ethics*, 2nd ed. (Oxford University Press, 1983), reprinted in Robert F. Weir, ed., *Ethical Issues in Death and Dying* (New York: Columbia University Press, 1986), p. 265.
11. Americans Against Human Suffering, "The Humane and Dignified Death Act" (proposed referendum), January 1989.
12. Brian Bard, "Voluntary Suicide May Make California Ballot," *Christianity Today*, April 8, 1988, p. 50.
13. James Rachels, "Active and Passive Euthanasia," *The New England Journal of Medicine*, January 9, 1975, pp. 78–80, reprinted in Robert F. Weir, ed., *Ethical Issues in Death and Dying* (New York: Columbia University Press, 1986), p. 250.
14. The Hippocratic oath, in Richard A. Wright, *Human Values in Health Care* (New York, McGraw-Hill, 1987), p. 284.
15. Arthur Dyck, "Beneficent Euthanasia and Benemortasia," reprinted from Marvin Kohl, ed., *Beneficent Euthanasia* (Buffalo, N.Y.: Prometheus, 1975), in Robert F. Weir, ed., *Ethical Issues in Death and Dying* (New York: Columbia University Press, 1986), p. 278.

CRITICALLY ILL ADULTS AND THE "RIGHT TO DIE" 83

16. Quoted in Yale Kamisar, "Some Non-Religious Views Against Proposed 'Mercy Killing' Legislation," in *Child and Family*, vol. 10, nos. 1, 2, 3; 1971. Reprinted in group, Reprint Booklet Series, 1987, p. 34.
17. Yale Kamisar, pp. 34–39.
18. Mark Siegler, "The A.M.A. Euthanasia Fiasco," *The New York Times*, February 26, 1988, p. 23.

ADDITIONAL SOURCES

Withdrawing Treatment

Jane Brody, "Personal Health," *The New York Times*, September 21, 1989, p. B20.
Ronald E. Cranford, "The Persistent Vegetative State," *Hastings Center Report*, February/March 1988, pp. 27–32.
Ruth Macklin, *Mortal Choices* (Boston: Houghton Mifflin, 1987).
John Edward Ruark, et al., "Initiating and Withdrawing Life Support," *The New England Journal of Medicine*, January 7, 1988, pp. 25–30.
Peter Steinfels, "Counting Food and Water as Extraordinary Support," *The New York Times*, April 30, 1989, p. E8.

Euthanasia

Lisa Belkin, "Doctors Debate Helping the Terminally Ill Die," *The New York Times*, May 24, 1989, p. A1.
Derek Humphry, "Legislating for Active Voluntary Euthanasia," *The Humanist*, March/April 1988, pp. 10–12, 47.
Daniel Maguire, "Deciding for Yourself: The Objections," excerpt from *Death by Choice* (New York: Doubleday, 1974), reprinted in Robert F. Weir, ed., *Ethical Issues in Death and Dying* (New York: Columbia University Press, 1986).
Sidney H. Wanzer, et al., "The Physician's Responsibility Toward Hopelessly Ill Patients," *The New England Journal of Medicine*, March 30, 1989, pp. 844–49.
Robert F. Weir, ed., *Ethical Issues in Death and Dying* (New York: Columbia University Press, 1986).

ORGANIZATIONS

The following organizations provided some of the materials for this chapter. Contact them for further information.

In favor of the right to die:

Americans Against Human Suffering
P.O. Box 11001
Glendale, CA 91206

National Council on Death and Dying
250 W. 57th St.
New York, NY 10107

Opposed to the right to die:

International Anti-Euthanasia Task Force
The Human Life Center
University of Steubenville
Steubenville, OH 43952

Issues in Law & Medicine
National Legal Center for the Medically Dependent and Disabled
P.O. Box 1586
Terre Haute, IN 47808-1586

CHAPTER SEVEN

ORGAN TRANSPLANTS AND ECONOMICS

THE twentieth century has been a time of extraordinary inventions and discoveries. Many people believe that with our vast resources and technological know-how, we can solve any problem that confronts us. But in medicine these days our technological know-how is outpacing our resources, and that is *creating* problems.

Scientists continue to improve high-tech methods, such as organ transplantation, for keeping people alive. But because of their expense, many patients do not have access to them. We face spiraling health-care costs and government budget crunches. We also confront a shortage of organs donated for transplantation. In this chapter we will examine the ethics of organ transplants in a time of scarcity.

MEDICAL ETHICS

...S FOR SALE?

...yone is born with two kidneys. These organs, located near the spinal column, excrete bodily wastes, which pass out of the body in our urine. If someone's kidneys fail as a result of injury or disease, he must get either dialysis or a kidney transplant, or he will die. The first successful organ transplant was performed thirty-five years ago by doctors in Boston—a kidney was transferred between identical twins. Since then there have been great advances in the procedure. But while transplant technology has made survival possible for people with renal (kidney) disease, there are not enough spare kidneys to go around.

Of all the bodily organs, kidneys are most commonly donated for transplant because many people want them, and because you need only one to live. A kidney transplant patient must take immunosuppressive drugs for his whole life, so his body does not reject the foreign organ, but otherwise he can live normally. A heart or liver for a transplant can come only from a cadaver, but you can give a kidney while you're alive and still live a normal life span. And donating a kidney involves little risk: the removal of the organ causes serious medical complications in only one case out of a thousand, death in only one case in five thousand.

The only alternative to a kidney transplant is dialysis, in which a machine does the work of the kidneys. The process is confining—it requires the patient to be hooked up to equipment for hours at a time three days a week. And as we saw in Chapter 3 in our discussion of Karen, the sixteen-year-old with kidney failure, the procedure can have devastating side effects for some people.

In the United States we would need four times as many donor kidneys as we currently have to satisfy the needs of renal disease patients. Selling bodily organs is illegal in this country, so kidneys must be freely donated. In 1987 three thousand U.S. citizens donated one of their kidneys to a family member. This accounted for one-third of all such transplants. The other kidneys came from the cadavers of people who had previously pledged to give their organs or whose families had given permission for the procedure.

In countries where a market in kidneys is available, people who are sick and have money can purchase kidneys from people who are healthy and poor. Proponents of this system say that as in all free trade, both sides end up better off. For instance, in 1988 a British man paid a Turkish citizen $3,300 to travel to Britain and donate a kidney. The donor needed the money for his daughter's medical care.

People opposed to these arrangements say they are fundamentally unfair. They benefit wealthy patients at the expense of those who are so desperate for money that they'll go under the knife.

In some parts of the world this opposition has carried the day. The Turkish kidney case made headlines in England, and Parliament subsequently banned the sale of human organs—joining at least twenty other countries with similar prohibitions. Though the practice is illegal in the United States (punishable by five years in jail and a $50,000 fine), Canada, and most of Western Europe, it is growing around the world. Brazil, the Philippines, and India, for instance, permit such trading in human parts for profit.

The continuing shortage of kidneys creates pressure on governments to allow a market in organs. Joel L. Swerdlow, who has written a report on the subject for a public-policy research group, says the benefits to organ recipients justify the buying of kidneys: "The altruistic 'gift relationship' may be inadequate as a motivator and an anachronism in medicine today. If paying seems wrong, it may nevertheless be preferable to accepting the suffering and death of patients who cannot otherwise obtain transplants."[1]

Rainer Scherer, a German organ broker, told *Newsweek* that benefits to the donor also justify the selling of organs: "Which is better: for me to give a poor guy 20,000 marks, or for him and his two healthy kidneys to be thrown onto the corpse cart after he starves?"[2]

Others say that preventing someone from doing what he wants with his body—in this case having a kidney removed—violates his autonomy. If you benefit someone, it may justify violating his autonomy. But if organ donation is the only way a person can get money to feed his children, it is hard to argue that legal barriers are a benefit to him. As medical lawyer Lori B. Andrews puts it, "Society has not benefited individuals by banning organ sales unless it also provides a means to escape desperate conditions."[3]

People opposed to organ selling worry that a donor can be coerced by a buyer, losing his autonomy. They point to cases of outright abuse. In one an Indian woman seeking a kidney transplant came to Britain with a male donor who said he was her cousin.[4] But the papers establishing their relationship turned out to be fake—and the donor was actually an employee of the woman's husband, who was a merchant. The merchant had threatened to fire the man if he did not sell a kidney to his wife. After the transplant had been performed, the donor came back to the clinic, complaining that he had been cheated: the merchant would not pay for the organ.

Aside from questions involving the individuals who participate in an organ-for-money deal, does allowing this trade have a negative effect on society at large? Writer Michael Kinsley worries that it does, by increasing the power of the rich. When organs are for sale, ill people with money can save themselves; those without it may not be able to. The wealthy already have access to many things to which the poor do not, but in a just society "the influence of money is not allowed to dominate all aspects of life."[5]

In his book *The Gift Relationship* Richard Titmuss discusses the many benefits to society of programs in which people donate blood for free—out of altruism, rather than to receive payment. People who believe organs should be similarly volunteered make an argument like his: such donations are a "small testament to our shared humanity."[6]

Almost all of the blood donated in the United States is given for free, and the supply is usually sufficient. The same cannot be said of organs. If organ-sale opponents are to be successful, they may need to come up with an alternative way of getting people to donate. Some have suggested a policy in which doctors would automatically remove organs for donation when a person died. If you did not want to donate your organs, you would have to make a formal request. This has been tried in Belgium, but it has not been effective. On moral rather than legal grounds, doctors there have resisted removing organs from a body without getting family permission.

TRANSPLANTS AND HEALTH CARE RATIONING

In 1987 the state legislature in Oregon decided to stop funding organ transplants for Medicaid patients and to use the money instead for programs, such as prenatal health care, that would benefit a larger number of people. One person directly affected by this decision was Sheila Holladay. The following is an excerpt from an essay she published in Family Circle *magazine.*

"When my younger son, David, was 10 months old, he came down with a fever. After performing tests ... the physician identified the problem. 'Your son has leukemia,' he said.

" ... my energies turned to understanding [the] disease. ... A child like David has, on the average, about two years to live. I learned about bone-marrow transplantation, the only weapon medicine has to fight this killer. And I learned a lot—far more than I wanted to, I am sad to say—about the price of a child's life.

"When David got sick, I was raising three kids, without a job, child support or medical insurance. I had almost no savings. I certainly couldn't pay for a transplant, which costs about $125,000. ...

" ... it had been almost a year, and his spleen became swollen. He barely had energy to crawl. His skin was so fragile that I used cotton balls to pat him dry. Finally, one day I broke down in front of one of his doctors: 'What am I going to do with my poor baby?' I cried.

"'Get him out of here,' he replied. ... 'go somewhere where you *can get funding for a bone-marrow transplant. If you stay here in Oregon, he'll die.'"**

Holladay did leave the state with her children, traveling by trailer to neighboring Washington—which funds organ transplants. But her baby died before a suitable donor could be found. Her story raised an uproar and sparked debate on a very troubling issue in medical ethics: How are limited resources to be allocated?

Whenever a government sets a budget, it is making a decision about resource allocation. Tax dollars are limited, and distributing them toward defense and roadways, for example, means less money is available for other endeavors like education and the environment. Health care is an item like any other in government budgets. State legislatures and the U.S. Congress fund health care through programs like Medicaid—which pays for medical services, usually including organ transplants, for people on low incomes.

Out of all the money that is available for health needs, governments must decide what types of care should be covered. The Oregon legislators made the controversial decision not to fund organ transplants. Their reasoning was that other, more widely beneficial health programs that were underfunded should get the money—tax dollars should be used to advance the greatest good for the greatest number of people. In ethics terms this reasoning is known as *utilitarianism.*

Utilitarianism often conflicts with ethical reasoning based on a person's individual rights, such as his right to autonomy or his right to health care. It focuses on what is good for society as a whole, rather than on what is good for an individual. In taking the utilitarian approach Oregon decided that improving health care for the general public was more important than satisfying the individual rights or needs of people like David Holladay. This approach dictated that health care must be rationed.

*Reprinted from the August 15, 1989 issue of *Family Circle* magazine. Copyright © 1989 THE FAMILY CIRCLE, INC.

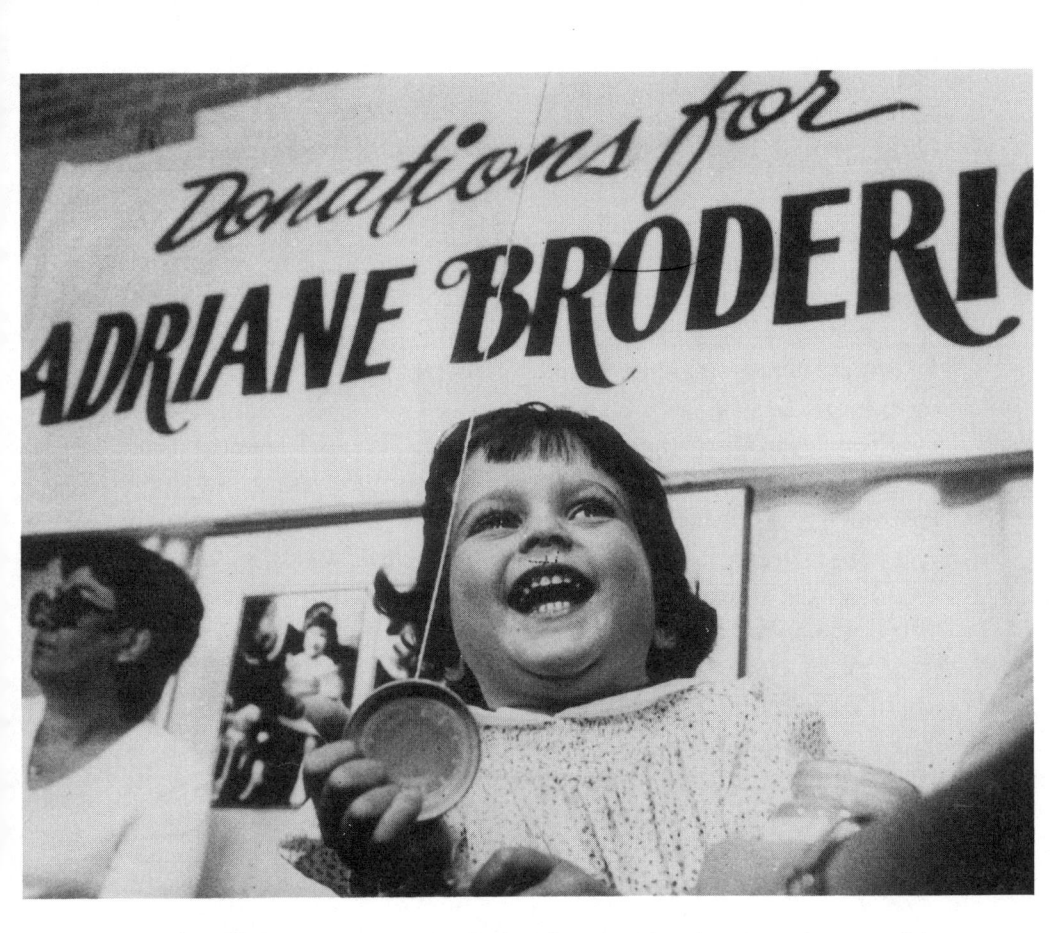

People all over the country helped raise the $65,000 that would allow 2-year-old Adriane Broderick to get on the waiting list for a liver transplant. Without the transplant, she would not survive.

Organ transplants are very expensive and they benefit relatively few people. Before setting its new policy, Oregon had paid for twenty-one heart, liver, and bone-marrow transplants at a cost of $1.15 million in state and federal funds. Many of the recipients died within a few years of their transplants.

The state has created a new health commission to help decide on health care priorities. Unofficial committees that previously took up this issue ranked birth control and abortion, and preventive medicine such as prenatal care, nutrition, and immunizations as some of the areas most deserving of funds; cosmetic surgery and organ transplants, on the other hand, were low priorities.

Many people are uncomfortable with the idea of turning our backs on patients in need of transplants. "You can't approach medicine merely as the greatest good for the greatest number of people," says Oregon legislator Tom Mason. "If we do that, why should anyone take care of you after a horrendous traffic accident?"[7]

Cory Franklin, chairman of the Division of Critical Care Medicine at Cook County Hospital in Chicago, points out that a utilitarian approach is discriminatory because it unfairly punishes—sometimes by death—poor people with illnesses that require costly treatment. Franklin says that rather than refuse to fund transplants, the government should find ways to decrease transplant costs.[8]

In a Harris poll taken in 1987 more than 90 percent of those questioned endorsed the concept that "everybody should have the right to get the best possible health care—as good as the treatment a millionaire gets."[9] A 1988 Gallup poll commissioned by *Hippocrates* magazine found that 76 percent of Americans oppose using "ability to pay" as a criterion for deciding who should be eligible for transplants when donor organs are scarce.

We seem, however, to be unwilling to put our wallets where our hearts are. Thirty-seven million people in this country have no medical insurance. Yet, according to a survey by the Public Agenda Foundation, only one out of ten people would be willing to pay $125 more in taxes to finance a national health insurance program—the kind of fiscal commitment that may be necessary to meet the needs of the David Holladays of the world. The reluctance to make this kind of sacrifice may account for the fact that after much debate over the issue in Oregon, only 15 percent of state residents favored transplant funding, 45 percent opposed it, and 40 percent were not sure—in a March 1989 survey published in the *Western Journal of Medicine*.

Health care costs are already rising at a rate of more than 15 percent a year. This makes it harder and harder to fund unlimited medical treatment. Because of this reality, proponents of rationing believe it is the only realistic and fair solution. They say opposition to the utilitarian approach is often hypocritical: while we are outraged at stories like the death of David Holladay, we accept a high infant-mortality rate, which stems largely from inadequate prenatal care.

Why is this? In part it is because people who need transplants are identifiable and visible as individuals—some even use the media to solicit financial donations; if they die, there is a specific cause. On the other hand, infants who die because they received poor prenatal care are perceived as mere statistics. They are not identifiable, and the inadequate care they were given is a much less direct cause of death. Yet there may be twenty such babies for every David Holladay.

It is easy to identify with Sheila Holladay's plight, while it is difficult indeed to feel for a "statistic." But as professor of medicine Leslie S. Rothenberg asks, "Is the human tragedy and the personal anguish of death from the lack of an organ transplant any greater than that of an infant dying in an intensive-care unit from a preventable problem brought about by a lack of prenatal care?"[10]

If economic realities force us to choose between supporting transplants and paying for prenatal care, another question is raised. Why should wealthy people be given access to transplants when poor people are not? As we have pointed out, the wealthy already can get many things that are unavailable to the poor. In this country, however, they cannot pay others for their organs. Should they also be barred from using their economic power to pay for operations not available to the less well-off? This question highlights a conflict in our ideals, as stated by Lester Thurow:

> A new expensive treatment is developed. In accordance with capitalistic principles, the wealthy are allowed to buy the treatment privately regardless of its medical effectiveness. Persons with a moderate or low income who cannot privately afford the treatment want it. They demand it. Being egalitarians, we have to give the treatment to everyone or deny it to everyone;

being capitalists, we cannot deny it to those who can afford it. But since resources are limited, we cannot afford to give it to everyone either.[11]

This is where the issue of rationing meshes with that of the buying and selling of organs. As long as organ sales are illegal, there is pressure for adopting an egalitarian system in which transplantation is funded for the less well-off. This is because most transplant organs come from cadavers and are donated—by rich and poor alike—to anyone who might need them. If funding enabling the poor to afford the transplant operation is denied, they might become resentful. Why should they benefit the wealthy when the wealthy will not help them? They could refuse to donate their organs.

Thus, unless transplants are supported financially by the government, it is possible that very few people would be able to get the operations under our current system. If they are not funded and organs become more scarce as a result, pressure might increase to legalize a free market in organs.

NOTES

1. Terry Trucco, "Sales of Kidneys Prompt New Laws and Debate," *The New York Times*, August 1, 1989, p. C1.
2. "Kidneys for Sale: The Issue Is Tissue," *Newsweek*, December 5, 1988, p. 38.
3. Lori B. Andrews, "My Body, My Property," *Hastings Center Report*, October 1986, p. 32.
4. William Boly, "For Sale: Used Kidney, Gd. Cond. $24K or Best Offer," *Hippocrates*, May/June 1988, p. 50.
5. Michael Kinsley, "Take My Kidney, Please," *Time*, March 13, 1989, p. 88.
6. Titmuss discussed in Thomas H. Murray, "Gifts of the Body and the Needs of Strangers," *Hastings Center Report*, April 1987, pp. 34–36; and in Michael Kinsley, "Take My Kidney, Please."
7. John Elson, "Rationing Medical Care," *Time*, May 15, 1989, p. 86.
8. Cory Franklin, "Commentary," *Hastings Center Report*, December 1988, pp. 35–36.
9. John Elson, pp. 84, 86.

10. Leslie S. Rothenberg, "Commentary," *Hastings Center Report,* December 1988, p. 34.
11. Quoted in John C. Moskop, "The Moral Limits to Federal Funding for Kidney Disease," *Hastings Center Report,* April 1987, p. 15.

ADDITIONAL SOURCES

Paul Cotton, "Transplants Bear the Brunt of Concern over Rationing," *Medical World News,* April 24, 1989.

Oscar Salvatierra, Jr., "Optimal Use of Organs for Transplantation," *The New England Journal of Medicine,* May 19, 1988, pp. 1329–1331.

Barney Speight, "Commentary," *Hastings Center Report,* December 1988, pp. 36–37.

"Where Americans Draw the Line," *Hippocrates,* May/June 1988, pp. 40–41.

Confidentiality is an important aspect of medical care. It gives patients dignity and furthers their autonomy by enabling them to control personal information. It also serves a practical medical purpose: people are often embarrassed by their medical conditions, and if they had to worry about doctors gossiping to others, it could discourage them from seeking treatment or being completely frank.

The right to confidentiality is protected by every ethical code in the medical profession and by law. For instance, in many states the information someone reveals to his or her doctor is considered privileged, and it cannot be used as evidence in court proceedings unless the patient agrees. Physicians who inappropriately repeat confidential material—whether in hospital corridors or on the golf course—are subject to lawsuits by patients and disciplinary action by peers.

The ethical codes of the American Psychiatric Association and the American Medical Association allow doctors to violate someone's confidentiality if the patient poses a danger to the public, as Poddar did. While these mandates give health care practitioners broad discretion to decide when revealing confidential information is appropriate, *Tarasoff* has made such disclosures a legal obligation. "Protective privilege ends where the public peril begins," said the court.[1] Although the case was decided in a California state court, it has become a precedent for other states as well.

George E. Dix explains the logic of *Tarasoff* this way:

> Therapists are in a unique position because they can foresee extremely dangerous conduct on the part of their patients. Consequently, the law should provide an incentive for them to anticipate such conduct, and, when it is anticipated, to take reasonable steps to prevent it. If therapists fail to exercise reasonable care to prevent assaultive acts by their patients, they should bear at least part of the financial responsibility for the patients' conduct.[2]

But many therapists say that the ruling ultimately fails to accomplish its goal—the protection of the public—and they call for laws to reverse it. Some argue that therapy is the best way to help a patient control aggressive impulses. Effective therapy demands a proper therapist–patient relationship, which requires that confidentiality not be compromised.

Jerome Beigler notes that survey results show "a significant erosion in the psychiatrist–patient relationship" since *Tarasoff*.[3] He says that some people with violent fantasies who need therapy avoid treatment or abandon it out of fear their doctors will breach confidentiality. Others will not reveal their aggressive impulses to their doctors, making effective therapy impossible. At the same time, observers believe that many therapists won't treat dangerous patients out of fear of *Tarasoff*-type lawsuits. And they worry that if people do not get needed treatment, they will pose a greater danger to society.

Another problem is the difficulty of predicting accurately who will actually use violence. Many, if not all, people have violent fantasies at times—and discuss them with their therapists—but relatively few act them out. Therapists may begin to disclose patients' threats too readily in order to protect themselves from legal action.

The tendency is illustrated well by an anecdote reported in *Hippocrates* magazine. A patient seeing a psychiatrist expressed "hostile feelings" toward a former boss. The patient had left the job long ago, and the boss had moved three thousand miles away; yet the psychiatrist reported the patient. "Because the supervisor worked for the Navy, the FBI was called in and the patient faced arrest on charges of threatening a federal employee."[4]

Despite all these objections, we must remember that Tatiana Tarasoff was killed, and that had she been warned, she might have avoided this fate. The Berkeley clinic upheld an important principle by not breaching confidentiality, but Tarasoff involuntarily paid a high price for this. It did not help her that patients could count on clinic psychotherapists to keep their secrets to themselves.

The "duty to warn" problem arises in other medical situations. The AIDS crisis has given the issue special urgency.

AIDS—acquired immune deficiency syndrome—weakens the body's immune system, which normally fights off diseases. As a result people with AIDS are vulnerable to a range of deadly illnesses, including pneumonia and cancer. The disease is spread primarily by unprotected sexual contact, sharing hypodermic needles, and blood transfusions.

All people with AIDS have been infected with HIV (human immune deficiency virus), the AIDS virus. But *not* all people with HIV have AIDS. Some people test positive for HIV but are otherwise healthy—they have none of the debilitating or fatal symptoms associated with AIDS. They may, however, be able to transmit the virus to others. People who are HIV-positive may go for years without symptoms; experts generally agree that most of them, however, will eventually develop full-blown AIDS and die.

How should a physician handle a patient with HIV who may spread the virus to others? The *Hastings Center Report* presented this scenario as an example of the dilemma:[5] A 28-year-old man, Mr. B, tests positive for HIV. He has no symptoms, but he could probably spread the virus. His doctor tells him how to avoid transmitting the virus: do not share hypodermic needles or donate blood; always use a condom during sex.

Mr. B then tells the doctor that he thinks he contracted HIV during sexual contact with another man. Further, he is now engaged to a woman, and he refuses to risk ruining his marriage plans by revealing his diagnosis to her. Should the doctor tell the fiancée of B's medical status and warn her that she may be at risk of developing AIDS through sexual contact with him? Or should he protect his patient's confidentiality?

Mr. B's refusal presents a dilemma similar to the one in the Tarasoff case. Morton Winston, chairman of the department of philosophy and religion at Trenton State College, says that because of uncertainty over the risks of HIV transmission, doctors should not be legally required to warn sexual partners in this situation. Instead, doctors should have discretion to decide what to do on a case-by-case basis.

The doctor, says Winston, must balance his obligation to

protect Mr. B's confidentiality against harm that could come to his fiancée and any future children they might have. He should try to convince his patient to tell the fiancée, and also make an offer, through Mr. B, to provide the woman with AIDS testing and counseling. What if Mr. B *still* will not go along? In that case, if the doctor determines "that the risk to his patient's fiancée is significant, and if all other means of persuading the patient to accept his moral responsibility have failed, then the doctor should attempt to contact her."[6]

Professor of medicine Sheldon H. Landesman is more reluctant to have Mr. B's doctor tell the fiancée. He argues that the availability of voluntary and confidential HIV testing is crucial to controlling the AIDS epidemic. "The expectation is that many, if not most, people who discover they are infected will behave appropriately by informing their partners and practicing safer sex."

If people worried that test results were not confidential, it would discourage them from getting tested in the first place. As a result they would not find out whether they had the virus or not, and neither would their sex partners. True, it might be painful for the doctor to ignore the plight of Mr. B's fiancée, "But his discomfort and the woman's infection may be the cost that society pays if it wishes to implement public health measures to minimize the spread of the virus."[7]

The "duty to warn" paradox, in Landesman's words, "is one of balancing long-term societal benefits against short-term benefit to an individual." If this seems like morally familiar territory at this point, that is because we looked at a similar conundrum in the last chapter. Like the *Tarasoff* case, the debate over health care rationing pits social utility against individual needs. Just as Tatiana Tarasoff was not warned about Poddar in order to preserve a broader social good—patient confidentiality—so was Sheila Holladay's child shut out from getting a lifesaving transplant to meet a societal need, funding for more widely beneficial forms of health care.

DOCTORS' RESPONSIBILITIES TO AIDS PATIENTS

In 1983 at Johns Hopkins University Hospital in Baltimore, Venezuelan-born doctor Hacib Aoun was caring for a teenager named Matthew who had leukemia. Matthew had gone through the usual treatments for his disease, including multiple transfusions. The incident that was to change Aoun's life is described in the magazine Hippocrates:

"*It was a routine procedure called a hematocrit, a test Aoun had performed hundreds of times. He first siphoned some of Matthew's blood into a thin, hollow, toothpick-sized glass vessel called a capillary tube. Then he sealed one end with a soft, puttylike plug so that he could spin the tube in a centrifuge. Aoun pushed down on the plug, unaware that it had hardened. The fragile tube snapped, and a jagged glass shaft rammed deep into Aoun's right index finger. . . .*"*

Over the next few years Aoun suffered from puzzling symptoms including fever, headaches, rashes, swollen lymph glands, and fatigue. Although Aoun hadn't known it when he did the hematocrit, Matthew had been exposed to the AIDS virus during his transfusions. On Christmas Eve, 1986, Aoun got back results of his own AIDS test—and discovered that now, through contact with Matthew's blood, he too had been exposed.

Before the widespread use of antibiotics in the 1940s, doctors always faced the risk of catching a fatal infectious disease from their patients. After that, doctors for the most part had not confronted this possibility for several decades. But since the advent of AIDS in the early 1980s, the possibility that they could contract the AIDS virus from a patient has been a daily concern for many of the doctors, nurses, lab technicians, ambulance drivers, paramedics, dentists, and others who make up the 6.8 million health professionals in the nation.

*Excerpted from Stephen S. Hall, "The Doctor," *Hippocrates*, May/June 1988, p. 74.

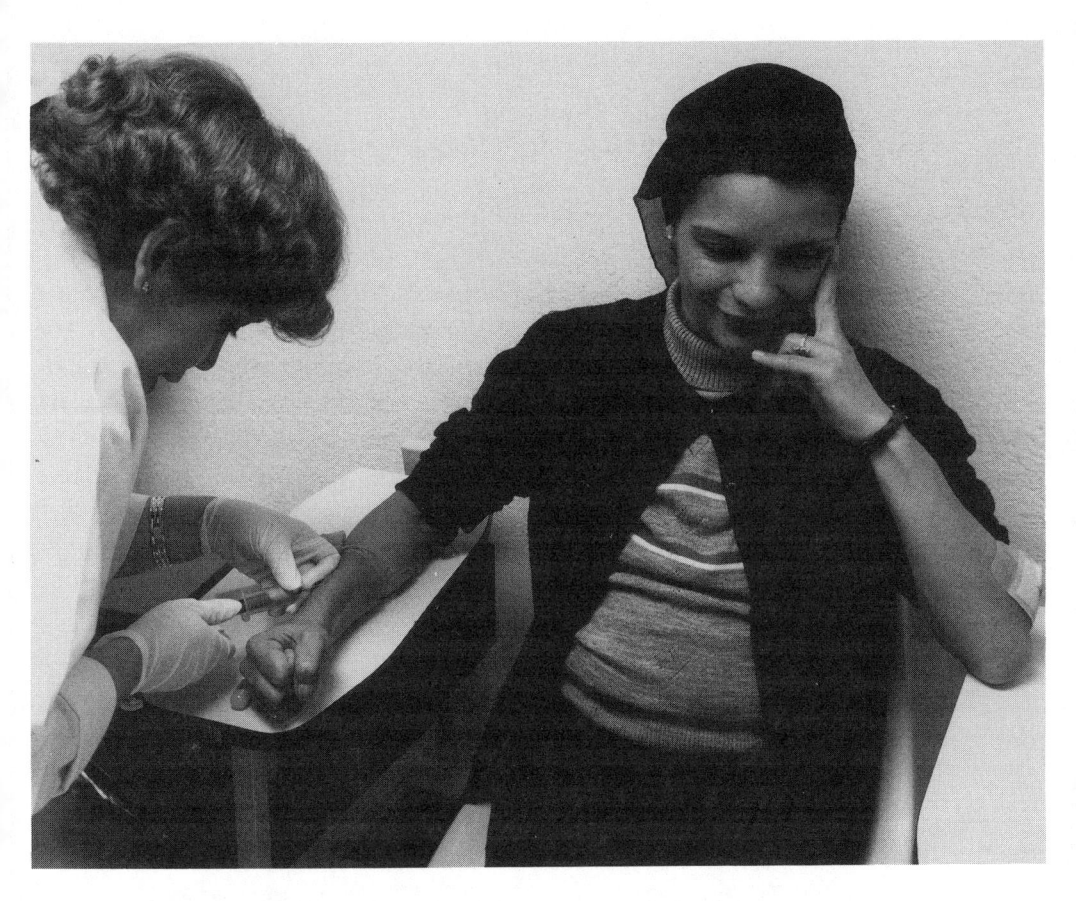

Drawing blood from a patient who has AIDS poses a certain amount of risk for health care workers.

Some health care workers have been reluctant to treat people who they know or suspect have HIV infection or full-blown AIDS. For example:

- Some doctors have refused care to people in high-risk groups, such as homosexuals and intravenous drug users, although the individuals involved were not known to have AIDS symptoms or to be HIV-infected.

- In Los Angeles a suit was brought against two paramedics who allegedly refused to help a man having a heart attack because they thought he had AIDS.

- Bioethicist Arthur Caplan says he is aware of medical students who do not want to care for people with AIDS and of dentists and nursing homes that will not take them as patients.

Few physicians publicly admit that they will not treat HIV-infected individuals. But in a survey of doctors in two highly regarded medical centers in New York City, 25 percent of those who responded said they would not care for AIDS patients if they did not have to, 34 percent felt they should have a choice in the matter, and 24 percent thought turning down AIDS patients was ethically acceptable. Do health care providers have the right to refuse to treat people with AIDS, or are they obligated to treat them?

A health care worker's chances of contracting the AIDS virus on the job are very small. Most cases are caused by accidental injury such as a doctor sticking herself with a needle that had been used on a patient. The Centers for Disease Control reported, however, that a few health care workers have contracted HIV merely from getting infected blood on their skin or mucous membranes (e.g., mouth, eyes).

The risk is somewhat greater for obstetricians and surgeons. During labor and delivery an obstetrician handles a liter or more of blood and amniotic fluid. So far at least twenty-one U.S. health-care workers and five health workers outside the nation have contracted the AIDS virus on the job.

Historically, doctors have a mixed record during epidemics. In 1348 many doctors left Venice, Italy, or stayed in their homes rather than treat bubonic plague victims in that city—100,000 people died. On the other hand, that same year the entire faculty of the medical school in Montpellier, France, bravely fought the plague—and *they* all died.

According to Daniel M. Fox, in the majority of epidemics most doctors have tended to the ill, but they often required higher pay as compensation for the risk they were taking.[8] Abigail Zuger and Steven H. Miles note that from the 1850s onward, bravery in medicine was the rule: "The stories of the cholera pandemics of the 19th century, the plague in the Orient, the influenza pandemic of 1918, polio in the 1950s, are largely ones of medical heroism."[9]

Today doctors are under no legal obligation to accept any particular person as a patient. Once a relationship with a patient has begun, doctors are not allowed to abruptly end it; but they can fulfill their legal duties merely by giving the patient reasonable notice and a referral to another doctor. It is unlawful, however, for doctors in emergency rooms to refuse treatment to anyone with a medical emergency. Besides these, several other legal and ethical rules govern health care providers who want to refuse to treat someone specifically because he or she has the AIDS virus.

Health maintenance organizations (HMO's), groups of physicians offering prepaid medical service, may be obligated to care for members who contract HIV. In most cases the monthly or yearly fee patients pay to an HMO guarantees that all services will be available to them. Also, many states and cities have laws barring discrimination against people with physical handicaps, including AIDS. Some of these laws apply to medical care. And several cities in California have passed statutes specifically protecting HIV carriers and people with AIDS from discrimination in getting health care.

Finally, each state has a medical licensing board to regulate the practice of medicine and license doctors. A doctor who violates a board's regulations can lose his or her license or have it suspended. These boards have taken two approaches. Licensing boards in some states, such as New Jersey, have issued regulations prohibiting doctors from arbitrarily refusing to treat people who are HIV-positive or who have AIDS. In other states, such as Arizona, the board permits doctors to refuse to treat such patients.

In addition to these legal considerations, a doctor's approach to AIDS patients may be governed by the codes of ethics followed by various medical groups. While such codes are not legally binding, those who violate them can lose membership in the organization. The Texas Medical Association, for instance, says it is ethically permissible for a doctor to refer patients with HIV if she would rather not treat them. A more mainstream position is taken by the American Nurses Association's Committee on Ethics, which issued a statement in 1986 saying that nurses are morally obligated to care for people with AIDS.

In 1987 the American Medical Association's Council on Ethical and Judicial Affairs declared: "A person who is afflicted with AIDS needs competent, compassionate treatment. Neither those who have the disease nor those who have been infected with the virus should be subjected to discrimination based on fear or prejudice, least of all by members of the health care community."[10] The public apparently agrees strongly with positions like this one. In a 1988 Gallup poll commissioned by *Hippocrates* magazine, by an almost two-to-one margin those surveyed did not think doctors should be able to turn down AIDS patients.

But doctors who do not want to treat people with HIV or AIDS believe that the risk they face is too high. Dudley Johnson, an internationally known heart surgeon working at St. Mary's Hospital in Milwaukee, specializes in removing cholesterol deposits and clots from heart arteries and then reconstructing the arteries using veins from the patient's legs. During the operation, which can take eight to twelve hours, blood seeps under his surgical gloves and sprays his face.

He told *Hippocrates* he would operate in emergencies and probably do routine bypass operations for patients infected with HIV. "But I'm not going to do a long, complicated, difficult procedure."[11]

James Mann, the chairman of the Texas Medical Association Board of Counselors, supports doctors like Johnson: "I don't think it can be called discrimination [against people with AIDS] when it's a matter of a guy laying his health and career on the line. A young man may spend 15 years of his life getting medical training and risk his life treating disease. You must think of the potential dangers and risks. . . . All it takes is a slip of a needle or a splash of secretions."[12]

And even if the fear of contracting AIDS is not always

rational, it is nevertheless real, argues James Kalivas, a doctor at the University of Kansas Medical Center in Kansas City. "You cannot command people not to be afraid. Fear is not logical and does not take orders. No one ... can condemn a doctor for not taking on a patient with AIDS ... if that action truly stems from fear."[13]

Many observers, though, believe there is no excuse for not accepting patients because they have AIDS. Former U.S. Surgeon General C. Everett Koop called doctors who won't treat people with HIV a "fearful and irrational minority," and criticized their "unprofessional conduct" that "threatens the very fabric of health care in this country."[14] Even if risks are involved, some argue, doctors must accept them—partly because that's the commitment they make as professionals, and partly because they are obligated to reciprocate the privileges they receive when they are licensed.

"Society could not tolerate firemen and policemen who refused ever to risk their lives in doing their jobs," says medical lawyer George Annas. "Nor should it tolerate physicians who refuse to take risks in their practice."[15] Philosopher John Arras says that some doctors are reluctant to take the risk because they don't approve of the behavior of the groups most likely to get AIDS. They may be willing to treat a child who contracted the virus in the womb or through a blood transfusion, but homosexuals and intravenous drug users are a different story. These doctors violate "the duty to treat all patients with respect for their human dignity," regardless of their lifestyles or their illness, according to Arras.[16]

Many worry that if doctors insist on adopting a voluntary system—in which only those doctors who wanted to would treat people infected with HIV—it would result in a shortage of medical personnel available to care for them. Hacib Aoun, the doctor who contracted AIDS from a young leukemia patient, presented a plea in *Hippocrates* on behalf of those who share his disease to those who share his profession: "Do you know how that feels when you're a patient, to know that somebody doesn't want to take care of you? Doesn't want to come close to you?

That feels really bad. ... if you're going to be a physician, be it *completely.*"[17]

During the AIDS epidemic, is this asking too much? Even Dr. Ezekiel J. Emanuel, who urges fellow health care professionals to treat patients with AIDS, acknowledges that surgeons face a particularly high risk. One way to deal with this, he says, would be for them to perform only urgent procedures and to avoid certain elective operations.[18] Other observers believe that AIDS doctors, like physicians in epidemics throughout history, may require higher fees and other incentives to compensate them for their risk.

NOTES

1. Quoted in Martin Lakin, *Ethical Issues in the Psychotherapies* (New York: Oxford University Press, 1988), p. 134.
2. George E. Dix, "Tarasoff and the Duty to Warn Potential Victims," in Charles K. Hofling, ed., *Law and Ethics in the Practice of Psychiatry* (New York: Brunner/Mazel, 1981), p. 138.
3. Jerome Beigler, "Privacy and Confidentiality," in Charles K. Hofling, ed., *Law and Ethics in the Practice of Psychiatry* (New York: Brunner/Mazel, 1981), p. 83.
4. Clark Norton, "When Should Doctors Tell Your Secrets?" *Hippocrates*, May/June 1988, p. 78.
5. "AIDS and a Duty to Protect," *Hastings Center Report*, February 1987, p. 22.
6. Morton Winston, "Commentary," *Hastings Center Report*, February 1987, pp. 22–23.
7. Sheldon H. Landesman, "Commentary," *Hastings Center Report*, February 1987, p. 23.
8. Daniel M. Fox, "The Politics of Physicians' Responsibility in Epidemics: A Note on History," *Hastings Center Report (Special Supplement)*, April/May 1988, pp. 5–10.
9. Quoted in John D. Arras, "The Fragile Web of Responsibility: AIDS and the Duty to Treat," *Hastings Center Report (Special Supplement)*, April/May 1988, p. 14.
10. Quoted in George J. Annas, "Legal Risks and Responsibilities of Physicians in the AIDS Epidemic," *Hastings Center Report (Special Supplement)*, April/May 1988, p. 29.
11. Stephen S. Hall, "The Doctor," *Hippocrates*, May/June 1988, p. 80.
12. Quoted in George Annas, "Legal Risks ... ," p. 30.

13. James Kalivas, letter, *The New England Journal of Medicine*, January 12, 1989, p. 121.
14. Quoted in George Annas, "Legal Risks ... ," p. 26.
15. George Annas, "Legal Risks ... ," pp. 31–32.
16. John D. Arras, "The Fragile Web of Responsibility: AIDS and the Duty to Treat," *Hastings Center Report (Special Supplement)*, April/May 1988, pp. 17–18.
17. Stephen S. Hall, "The Doctor," *Hippocrates*, May/June 1988, p. 76.
18. Ezekiel J. Emanuel, "Do Physicians Have an Obligation to Treat Patients with AIDS?" *The New England Journal of Medicine*, June 23, 1988, pp. 1687, 1689.

ADDITIONAL SOURCES

The "Duty to Warn"

Leonard D. Goodstein, "Duty to Protect" (memorandum to the American Psychological Association, 1985).
Ruth Macklin, *Mortal Choices* (Boston: Houghton Mifflin, 1987).
Robert Veatch, *A Theory of Medical Ethics* (New York: Basic Books, 1981).

Doctors' Responsibilities to AIDS Patients

James R. Allen, "Health Care Workers and the Risk of HIV Transmission," *Hastings Center Report (Special Supplement)*, April/May 1988, pp. 2–5.
Taunya Lovell Banks, "The Right to Medical Treatment," in Harlon L. Dalton et al., eds., *AIDS and the Law* (New Haven: Yale University Press, 1987).
Benjamin Freedman, "Health Professions, Codes, and the Right to Refuse to Treat HIV-Infectious Patients," *Hastings Center Report (Special Supplement)*, April/May 1988, pp. 20–25.
"The HIV-Infected Patient Who Conceals His Condition," *Medical Economics*, April 3, 1989, pp. 19–20.
Michael Powell, "Dealing with the Risk at Work," *Newsday* (New York), January 10, 1990, pp. 4, 25.
"Where America Draws the Line," *Hippocrates*, May/June 1988, pp. 40–41.

CHAPTER NINE

RECURRING THEMES

WE have examined a wide range of topics in medical ethics. Several important moral principles and themes have recurred in our discussion of these issues.

Autonomy: Autonomy is your basic right to do as you please and be left alone, provided you do not interfere with the rights of others. This right prevents the state, or other individuals, from controlling your life. The right to autonomy has been invoked in numerous problems in medical ethics.

People favoring abortion rights say that every woman should have the autonomous choice to terminate her pregnancy. She, not the state or a doctor, has the right to control her own body. The same argument is made for teenagers who want access to abortion. Just because they are young is no reason to deny them autonomy in this situation; if they are old enough to get pregnant and decide to give birth, they are old enough to decide to get an abortion, say many prochoice activists.

The established right to refuse medical treatment is based on a person's autonomy. This is invoked by women who want to refuse cesarean sections that doctors or courts insist on for the benefit of the child. They argue that such operations are a violation, a form of assault when performed without consent.

Advocates for the "right to die" also use the idea of individual autonomy to support their cause. They ask, Whose life is it, anyway—the community's or the individual's? If it is the individual's life, as most people in a democracy believe, then it should be the individual's choice to end it. This is the ultimate autonomous decision.

In addition to individual autonomy, we have discussed family autonomy. This principle gives people the right to exert control over the medical care of family members who are not able to make their own decisions. Some parents claim family autonomy gives them the right to make medical decisions for their seriously ill underage children, whether they are teenagers or premature "Baby Does." This can cause clashes with the state when authorities believe those decisions are not in the children's best interests. And some people claim the right to make medical decisions for unconscious relatives—even the right to hasten their deaths—as discussed in the Nancy Cruzan case in Chapter 6.

Some of the issues in organ transplantation also involve the principle of autonomy. People who favor a free market in organs say that laws preventing this are a violation of autonomy. If someone feels it is in his interest to sell a kidney, he should be able to do so. The state should respect individuals and not try to protect them from themselves.

Finally, doctors who do not want to care for AIDS patients appeal to the principle of autonomy. They argue that it is their right to decide who to care for, as it is the patient's right to choose his own doctor.

Beneficence: This is one of the values that competes with autonomy. The moral imperative that a doctor should do no harm and always benefit his patient sometimes conflicts with the patient's right to control his care. A doctor may resist honoring a patient's "right to die" because he feels, say, that the patient may eventually recover from his illness or that his pain may subside. Allowing him to die in this situation by, for example, disconnecting life-support equipment would be an act of harm.

Beneficence is a particularly important principle when the patient has diminished autonomy. Because minors are not believed to have the full decision-making abilities adults do, legislatures, courts, and doctors are less apt to honor their autonomy. Instead, they try to benefit the child by pursuing his best interests. These authorities may require parental consent for a teenager to get an abortion, and they may require medical procedures to be performed against the wishes of the child and the parents. Whether or not this kind of paternalism actually does benefit the child is debatable, but these actions generally are taken in the name of beneficence.

Some people also say that this principle requires doctors to treat patients with AIDS regardless of the small risk to themselves and not to perform abortions, which would be harming the fetus.

Conflicting obligations: This refers to situations in which you owe some type of moral debt to two people whose interests clash. Satisfying your obligations to one person will mean hurting the other. The problem of conflicting obligations arises in reproductive issues, in which the autonomy of the mother is pitted against the well-being of her fetus.

Are doctors and the courts justified in forcing a woman to have a cesarean section against her will if that is necessary to ensure the health of her baby? Should abortion be legal? The basic question here is whether doctors and society are obligated to benefit and not harm the fetus and whether this obligation overrides their duty to honor a woman's autonomy.

Conflicting obligations are also involved in the "duty to warn" issue. Psychotherapists and doctors have an obligation to maintain the confidentiality of their patients. They also have an obligation to protect the public from patients who may be dangerous; to satisfy this duty, they may have to warn anyone who is endangered about the threat the patient represents. The duty to warn and the obligation to respect the patient by honoring his confidentiality are thus on a collision course.

Utilitarianism: The principle of utility requires us to do the greatest good for the greatest number of people. This principle is sometimes used as a justification for maintaining a patient's confidentiality even when he may harm a third party.

Should doctors warn the sex partners of people who test positive for AIDS? The utilitarian argument is that if confidentiality is not maintained, it will discourage people from getting tested in the first place. If people do not get tested, the disease will spread, harming large sections of the population. Therefore, the most utilitarian course of action is this: risk the possibility that an individual will contract AIDS as a result of sexual contact with your patient in order that ultimately, the wider population can be protected.

Utilitarianism also comes into play when legislatures decide not to fund organ transplants so that other, more widely beneficial health programs can be financially supported. Organ transplants are very expensive and they benefit relatively few people. Programs like prenatal care, on the other hand, help a large section of the population for relatively little money.

Finally, decisions to allow teenagers confidential access to birth control and abortion are sometimes based on utilitarian considerations. The reasoning is that teen pregnancy is a tremendous social problem. When teenagers have children it perpetuates a cycle of poverty, and it increases the amount of money the government must contribute to welfare programs. Making it easier for teenagers to avoid or terminate pregnancy may thus benefit society as a whole, which is utilitarianism's goal.

Whenever a medical ethics issue is in the headlines, it's up to you to sort out what values are at stake. As technology advances, new questions will be raised, but the underlying principles involved in ethics debates will remain the same. These moral imperatives, like the one commanding "Thou shalt not kill," are sometimes as old as civilization itself. Ask yourself what is the basis for arguments you hear made for or against abortion rights, euthanasia, health-care rationing, and other such issues. Is it autonomy, beneficence, utility? Do you find the arguments convincing? Are the values being appealed to appropriate to the question? Why or why not? This will help you get at the heart of some of the most dramatic and compelling issues of our time.

APPENDIX

LANDMARK COURT CASES

Belloti v. *Baird* (U.S. Supreme Court, 1979): The Court ruled that most minors (people under 18) have the right to choose abortion without parental consent. It suggested, though, that parental-consent laws involving abortion would be constitutional if they offered a "judicial bypass procedure." In this procedure a minor appears before a state judge to ask to be exempt from the consent requirement. If she can convince the judge either that she is mature enough to make the decision on her own or that asking her parents for permission is not in her best interests, the consent requirement is waived.

Webster v. *Reproductive Health Services* (U.S. Supreme Court, 1989): Without reversing *Roe* v. *Wade*, which gave all women in the United States the legal right to abortion, the Court allowed sharp state restrictions on the procedure. A 5–4 majority upheld a Missouri law that prohibits public hospitals from performing abortions not required to save the life of the mother; prohibits health care providers employed by the state from performing such abortions; and in cases in which the woman is at least twenty weeks pregnant, requires tests to be done on the fetus to determine if it is viable (can live outside the womb).

Angela Carder (District of Columbia Court of Appeals, 1990): Angela Carder, 26 weeks pregnant, was diagnosed with terminal lung cancer and told she had only a few days to live. The doctors thought they might have a responsibility to save her fetus—which they believed could live outside her body at this point—by performing a cesarean section. If she died first, the fetus's life would surely end with hers. Since she would not consent to the procedure, the hospital called in a judge to hear the case. The judge ordered a cesarean. After the procedure, the baby lived for just two hours; Carder died two days later. On appeal, the D.C. high court ruled that women's right to "bodily integrity" protected them against such forced surgery, and that right remained in force even when they were "at death's door."

Belchertown v. Saikewicz (Supreme Court of Massachusetts, 1977): Joseph Saikewicz was a 67-year-old man who was severely retarded, with a mental age near 3 years, and unable to talk. He suffered from incurable leukemia, and his doctors wanted to keep him alive with chemotherapy, which has many unpleasant side effects. His guardian asked that no treatment be given. The court ruled that people who are incompetent to make medical decisions have the same right to refuse treatment as others; the benefits of the proposed treatment were not worth the pain and fear it would cause Saikewicz, who would refuse the chemotherapy if he could.

Brother Fox (New York Court of Appeals, 1981): At age 83 Brother Fox, a monk, had a heart attack during an operation and lapsed into a state of permanent unconsciousness. His confessor testified that Fox had taught ethics and had discussed the case of Karen Quinlan with him. Fox had said that if he were ever in her condition, he would not want his life preserved by extraordinary measures. Accordingly, the confessor requested that Fox's respirator be removed. The court found Fox's words to be "solemn pronouncements and not casual remarks" and ordered the hospital to remove the respirator.

Mary O'Connor (New York Court of Appeals, 1988): A 77-year-old woman named Mary O'Connor had suffered several strokes that left her paralyzed and, according to doctors, "severely demented." Her hospital wanted to insert a feeding tube through her nose. O'Connor's two daughters refused, saying she had repeatedly told them before becoming ill that she would not want to be kept alive artificially if there were no chance of improvement.

LANDMARK COURT CASES

The hospital asked the court to order the feeding, and the court did so because O'Connor had not specifically said she would want to be deprived of food in this situation.

Bouvia v. *Superior Court of California* (California Court of Appeals, 1986): Elizabeth Bouvia, 28, was paralyzed below the neck, suffered from severe cerebral palsy, and was in constant pain. She asked a hospital to let her starve to death. The hospital refused, and when the staff decided she was not eating enough, force-fed her through a tube. She protested to the court, which ordered the hospital to comply with her wishes and remove the tube. It reasoned that her right to privacy allowed her to refuse care, regardless of her motives.

Moore v. *University of California* (California Court of Appeals, 1988): John Moore was treated for leukemia by a doctor at the University of California at Los Angeles. His spleen was removed, and his condition soon improved. Moore says that the doctor who took the organ used it to create a "cell line" that would produce medicine—and financial profit. He sued the doctor, the university, and others for allegedly doing this without his permission. The court of appeals said the lawsuit was legitimate and could go forward, ruling, "The essence of property interest—the ultimate right of control ... exists with regard to one's own body."

INDEX

Abortion, 2, 37–43, 61, 80, 110, 112, 113, 115
   case against legal rights, 43
   case for legal rights, 42–43
   history, 39
   Roe v. *Wade*, 14, 39–41
   teenage, 14–18
   Webster v. *Reproductive Health Services*, 16, 41, 43, 115–116
Adolescents *see* Teenagers
AIDS (acquired immune deficiency syndrome), 99–108, 111, 112, 113
Alan Guttmacher Institute, 38
Alcohol, 48
Alsop, Donald D., 18
American Association of Neurological Surgeons, 70
American Civil Liberties Union (ACLU), 16, 17
American Medical Association, 70, 79, 98, 106
American Nurses Association, 106
American Psychiatric Association, 98
Americans Against Human Suffering (AAHS), 76
Amish, 34
Andrews, Lori B., 88
Annas, George J., 46, 107
Antibiotics, 2

Aoun, Hacib, 102, 107
Arizona, 105
Armstrong, Paul, 73
Arras, John, 107
Artificial nutrition, 69–71, 74, 78, 116–117
Assisted suicide, 75–76
Autonomy, 5–7, 59, 65, 68, 88, 110–111, 112

Babies, critically ill, 57–63
Baby Doe case, 59–61, 62, 67
Battering, of women, 17
Bays, Jan, 49
Beigler, Jerome, 99
Belchertown v. *Saikewicz*, 116
Belloti v. *Baird*, 115
Belson, James A., 47
Beneficence, 5–7, 111–112
Bioethics, 3, 4, 90
   see also Health care; specific cases and issues
Birth control, 12–14, 42, 113
Blackmun, Harry, 43
Blacks, 2
Blood donors, 88
Blood transfusions, 27
Boston Women's Health Book Collective, 37
Bouvia v. *Superior Court of California*, 117
Brain death, 4
Broderick, Adriane, 91

119

Brother Fox case, 116
Bubonic plague, 104
Burden standard, 62

California, 48, 76–77, 105, 117
Callahan, Daniel, 69
Caplan, Arthur, 2, 104
Capron, Alexander Morgan, 12
Carder, Angela, 44, 46, 47, 116
Carey v. Population Services International, 14
Catholic Church *see* Roman Catholic Church
Centers for Disease Control, 104
Cesarean sections, 45–47, 111, 112, 116
Children
 critically ill babies, 57–63
 parents' control over, 23–25
 parents' refusal of treatment for, 27–29
 right to make decisions, 25–27
 see also Teenagers
China, 41, 42, 49
Civil rights, 61
Cleft palate, 31
Clouser, Danner, 4–5
Cole, James S., 71
Colen, B.D., 73
Confidentiality, 98, 100–101, 112, 113
Conflicting obligations, 7–8, 112–113
Contraceptives *see* Birth control
Coons, Carrie, 74
Crack cocaine, 45
Cruzan, Joe, 70
Cruzan, Nancy, 70–72, 74

Davis, Junior Lewis, 49–52
Davis, Mary Sue, 49–52
Dix, George E., 98
Doctor-patient relationship, 2–3, 80, 96–108
Down syndrome, 59, 62
Drugs, 45, 47–49
Duty to warn, 97–101
Dyck, Arthur, 79

Emancipated minors, 12
Emanuel, Ezekiel J., 108
Embryos, 50–53, 80
Emergencies, 105
Epidemics, 104–105
Ethics, definition of, 4
Euthanasia, 74–81

Feeding *see* Artificial nutrition
Fetal alcohol syndrome, 48
Fetal vs. maternal rights, 38–39, 44–49, 80, 116
Field, Martha A., 52–53
Florida, 48, 77
Fourteenth Amendment, 72
Fox, Daniel M., 104
France, 41
Frank, Hugh A., 62
Franklin, Cory, 92
French, Howard W., 58
Fundamentalists, 43

Gift Relationship, The, 88
Giorgi, Lori, 49
Goldstein, Joseph, 33
Gorovitz, Samuel, 5

INDEX

Green, Ricky Ricardo, 33–34
Griswold v. Connecticut, 14

Harelip, 31
Hastings Center Report, 100
Health care
  critically ill babies, 57–63
  euthanasia, 74–81
  history, 1–2
  moral values in, 1–9
  organ transplants, 85–94
  right-to-die issue, 64–81, 111, 112
  withdrawing treatment, 65–74
Health maintenance organizations (HMOs), 105
Hentoff, Nat, 43, 61
Hippocrates magazine, 48, 65, 92, 99, 102, 106, 107
Hippocratic oath, 5, 79
HIV (human immune deficiency virus), 100–101, 103–107
Hodgkin's disease, 29
Hodgson v. Minnesota, 16–18
Holladay, Sheila, 89–90, 93, 101
Humane and Dignified Death Act, 76–77
Humphry, Derek, 74–75
Humphry, Jean, 74–75

Incompetency, 66, 68, 71
Infants, premature, 58–60
In re Pogue, 27
In re Ricky Ricardo Green, 33–34
In re Sampson, 32–33
In re Seiferth, 30–32, 33
Insurance, 92
In-vitro fertilization, 49–53

Jehovah's Witnesses, 27–29, 33–34
Jehovah's Witnesses of Washington v. King County Hospital, 27–27
Jennings, Bruce, 74
Johnson, Dudley, 106

Kalivas, James, 107
Kamisar, Yale, 80
Kansas, 4
Kevorkian, Jack, 76
Kidney dialysis, 1, 2, 21–22, 24, 86
Kidney transplants, 86–87, 88
Kinsley, Michael, 88
Koop, C. Everett, 107

Lamkins, Donald, 71
Landesman, Sheldon H., 101
Laramie (Wyo.), 48
Laws
  abortion, 2
  fetal neglect, 48
  and medical ethics, 4
  parental-involvement, 14–17
  see also specific states
Liquid oxygen, 41
Living wills, 68, 72

Maguire, Daniel, 80
Maine, 72
Mann, James, 106
Mason, Tom, 92
Massachusetts, 23, 28
McCormick, Richard A., 61

Medicaid, 3, 89, 90
Medical care *see* Health care
Medical ethics *see* Bioethics
Medical insurance, 92
Medicare, 3
Mercy killing *see* Euthanasia
Miles, Steven H., 104
Minneapolis (Minn.), 16
Minnesota, 16–18
Minnesota Citizens Concerned for Life (MCCL), 16
Minor, Richard, 30
Minors *see* Children; Emancipated minors; Teenagers
Missouri, 70–72, 115
Moore, Lawrence, 97
Moore v. University of California, 117

National Right to Life organization, 43
Nazis, 80
Netherlands, 77
New Jersey, 105
New York State, 31, 72
Nonvoluntary euthanasia, 75
Nutrition *see* Artificial nutrition

Obstetricians, 104
O'Connor, Mary, 116
Ohio, 18
Oregon, 77, 89–92
Organ transplantation, 2, 85–94, 111
O'Rourke, Kevin, 71

Painkillers, 78–79
Parental-involvement laws, 14–17
Parents
  control over children, 23–25
  decision-making for children, 22–23
  disagreements with doctors, 29–30
  refusal of treatment for children, 27–29
  rights of, 23
Parness, Jeffrey A., 47
Paternalism, 5
Paul, Eve W., 49
Pennsylvania, 33–34
Persistent vegetative state (PVS), 66, 72–74
Placenta previa, 47
Poddar, Prosenjit, 97, 98, 101
Polio, 33
Poverty, 42
Pregnancy
  Cesarean sections, 45–47, 111, 112, 116
  in-vitro fertilization, 49–53
  surrogate mothers, 52–53
  teenage, 11–14
Premature infants, 58–60
Prince v. Massachusetts, 28
Privacy, 14, 16, 43, 59, 70
Protestant Fundamentalists, 43
Proxies, 68
Psychotherapy, 97–99, 112
PVS *see* Persistent vegetative state

Quality of life, 61–62, 65, 67, 71
Quinlan, Joseph, 67, 69
Quinlan, Karen Ann, 66–69, 116

INDEX

Rachels, James, 78
Reagan, Ronald, 41, 59
Religion, 3, 27–29, 33–34, 61
Reproduction, 36–53, 80
Respirators, 2, 57, 66, 69, 78, 116
Right-to-die issue, 64–81, 111, 112
Robertson, Edward, Jr., 71
Robertson, John A., 52
Roe v. Wade, 14, 39–41
Roman Catholic Church, 43, 51, 61
Rothenberg, Leslie S., 93
RU 486 (drug), 41

Saikewicz, Joseph, 116
Sampson, Kevin, 32–33
Sanctity of life, 60–61, 62, 67, 71
Scherer, Rainer, 87
Scientific experiments, 2, 80
Scully, Thomas and Celia, 25, 30
Secular ethics, 3, 61
Seiferth, Martin, Jr., 30–32, 33
Sexually transmitted diseases (STDs), 12
Siegler, Mark, 80
Singer, Peter, 51
Slippery slope argument, 79–80
Stewart, Pamela Rae, 47–48
Substituted judgment, 68
Suicide, 75–76
Supreme Court (U.S.), 14, 16–18, 25, 28, 34, 39–41, 72, 115
  see also specific cases
Surgeons, 104
Surrogate mothers, 52–53

Swerdlow, Joel L., 87
Syphilis, 2

Tarasoff, Tatiana, 97, 98, 99, 101
Teenagers, 1–34
  and abortion, 14–18
  and life-threatening illnesses, 21–30
  and non-life-threatening illnesses, 30–34
  pregnancy, 11–14
  right to make decisions, 25–27
Terminal illness, 65, 77–78, 80
Terry, John A., 47
Texas Medical Association, 105, 106
Thurow, Lester, 93
Titmuss, Richard, 88
Transplants *see* Organ transplantation
Travers, Mary, 42
Treatment withdrawal, 65–74

Ultrasonography, 44
Unconsciousness, 66, 71, 80
U.S. Public Health Service, 2
Utilitarianism, 90, 113

Violence, 99
Voluntary euthanasia, 75
Von Reckinghausen's disease, 32

Washington, 77
Webster v. Reproductive Health Services, 16, 41, 43, 115–116

Wells, Deane, 51
Willis, Ellen, 46
Wills *see* Living wills
Winston, Morton, 100

Young, W. Dale, 52

Zuger, Abigail, 104

Daniel Jussim, a graduate of Vassar College, is a freelance writer living in New York City. His previous book for Messner was *Drug Tests and Polygraphs: Essential Tools or Violations of Privacy?*